THE RAKEHELL'S SEDUCTION

The Seduction Series - Book 2

LAUREN SMITH

LAUREN SMITH
BOOKS

To Jessica F., Jennifer H., Sue G. and Kerri H. for your support and friendship as amazing ladies!

Lothbrook, England – September 1821

A mbrose Worthing was attending a country dance.

The notion was laughable. He, a glorified rakehell with a distaste for country life, was currently entrapped in a bloody assembly room that could pass for a barn on better days. In fact, as he glanced around the room, he decided it most certainly resembled a farmyard at the moment, with the gaggle of society mamas squawking like geese, their turbans festooned with tall ostrich plumes.

He groaned when he saw them scrutinizing him, whispering behind their fans, their eyes dancing over his form as they assessed his marital suitability. From the clever smiles he glimpsed, he knew they were ready to throw their innocent daughters at his feet.

Like bloody hell. He was not about to find himself accidentally "compromising" any of the young ladies here tonight. He'd come here tonight to find one particular young woman to seduce her, to win a bet he'd made in London the previous week, and hopefully save her. He was not about to let the gathering of society mamas intimidate him into dancing with their daughters, even if they rivaled the great ancient Mongolian Golden Horde led by Genghis Khan. Many a rake had fallen under their wiles, surfacing months later to find themselves stuck with a shy chit of a girl as a wife and an obnoxious mother-in-law.

At twenty-nine years old, he'd managed to weather many attempts by his friends and relatives to see him settled. If those who loved him could not bring him to the altar, no silly chits from the country would have any success either. He was a permanent bachelor, and he liked it. Marriage was not made for men like him. To be tied down with one woman for the rest of his life and suffer the trappings of home and hearth when he could be exploring the world and living? Heavens no, he would not give up his freedom for anything.

A few daring matchmaking mamas separated from the crowd and walked in his direction. Damnation, even the need for a master of ceremonies to perform introductions wouldn't stop these women.

Ambrose spun on his heel, desperate to avoid conversation. If he had to listen to one more story about how well their daughters played the pianofortes or how accomplished they were at needlepoint, he'd run from the assembly hall screaming.

He had met almost everyone present at the dance and had no desire to continue any of the acquaintances. He was only here because of the wager placed in a betting book at White's. A damned fool named Gerald Langley had put down in the books that anyone who plucked the fruit of this girl's vine would receive five thousand pounds from him. Langley was a brute with little in the way of good sense and far too much coin. Ambrose had no idea why Langley had it in for the Earl of Rockford's daughter, but he did. After reading the bet, Ambrose had penned his name to the challenge and notified Langley he had accepted the wager.

For once in his life he was trying to do the right thing by a woman. It was a bit ironic, though, that saving the woman required compromising her. But the Earl of Rockford and his father had been friends, and Ambrose felt he owed it to Rockford to win the wager and keep the lady safe from true scoundrels. No other man would take the care with her that he would and see to it that her first time with a man was a pleasurable experience.

He had one month to seduce Rockford's daughter and provide proof of this seduction in London. As the lady in question had never been to London, there was much speculation among the men at his club whether she was a diamond of the first water or a dowdy creature. The betting book listed her age as twenty-two, young enough not to be an ape leader, a nasty term for women nearing spinsterhood.

Apparently Rockford wasn't one for traditions. Any father wishing to ensure his daughter's future would have brought her to London at seventeen or eighteen, had her presented to the queen, and then made the round of balls to hunt for a husband.

Yet Rockford had not done any of that. He'd kept his daughter in the country, living a quiet life. An unplucked fruit to tempt the worst sort of men in White's to bet upon the taking of her maidenhead for their own amusement.

Normally Ambrose had little desire to compete in wagers, especially ones which involved the corruption of innocents. It was not out of some moral principle, but rather a dislike of virgins. They tended to fall in love and cling to the man who took their innocence. But after witnessing the sort of men discussing whether to take the bet that night, Ambrose decided he would do this inno-cent lady a favor. He'd penned his name in the books, taking up the wager, and sent a letter to Rockford, renewing their acquaintance.

A letter from Rockford arrived only a few days later, inviting Ambrose to this ball and to spend a few weeks at Rockford's home as a guest. It was the perfect opportunity for Ambrose to cozy up to the man's daughter and see what sort of creature he would soon be bedding.

If only he knew what the lady looked like. In the chaotic din full of dancing and music, he could not find a single young lady among the crush that he was willing to bed. It wasn't that the young ladies weren't attractive. They were, but none were to his taste. Innocent young ladies had never appealed to him. If his friend Gareth Fairfax had been there, Gareth would have been laughing at him. Gareth was stuck in his own hell—the poor fool was happily married. *Married!* Ambrose couldn't think of anything more terrifying than being stuck with one woman for the rest of his life. Helen was a darling creature and perfectly suited to Gareth, and Ambrose supposed it would be not too terrible to share a bed with a woman like her. But still, to be leg-shackled?

I would rather die in a thousand unspeakable ways than stand in a bloody church and tie myself to one woman for the rest of my days.

"Mr. Worthing! Oh, Mr. Worthing!" Mrs. Minerva Darby called out in a shrill voice.

Ambrose winced and fled, ducking around dancers caught up in a lively quadrille. He narrowly avoided colliding with two men as he fell into the shelter of a doorway leading to the back gardens. If there was one woman to fear above all others tonight at this country dance, it was Mrs. Darby, a particularly determined match-making mama. He suspected she was the sort of woman who would knock a man out with her parasol, drag him behind a bush, and throw her daughter upon him before "discovering" the couple and announcing an inevitable engagement.

He peered around the corner, relieved when he saw a clear path to escape her. If she knew anything of him at all, she would have locked her daughter away in the nearest tower and hired a fleet of fire-breathing dragons to guard her. But Ambrose's rakehell reputation had not yet reached Lothbrook. The town was small enough that he could take ten strides and would have traveled a good majority of the only stretch of road that could be called a street in this little village.

"Excuse me, have you seen Mr. Worthing?" Mrs. Darby's voice came perilously close to where he was concealed behind a tall bush in the gardens.

"Afraid not, madam. Perhaps he's visiting the gentlemen's antechamber," a man answered. Ambrose couldn't see him from his hiding spot. It was likely that the man didn't know him, but simply didn't wish to keep conversing with Mrs. Darby. The surest way to drive a woman off was for a man to mention seeing to nature's call. Ambrose couldn't help but chuckle at his good fortune.

Still, it would be safe not to linger too close to the doors leading back to the dancers, just in case Mrs. Darby thought to peek into the gardens and spied him hiding like a guilty lad behind the shrubbery.

With a hasty turn and quick steps, he came around the nearest corner of the bushes.

Whump!

He collided with someone else coming from the opposite direction.

Their bodies smacked together, and the second body let out a feminine gasp of pain. They toppled to the ground. In the dim light he couldn't clearly see the woman who lay beneath him. The woman's full breasts pressed against his ribs, and the scent of rosewater teased his nose.

"Would you—mind terribly...I cannot breathe." The woman panted beneath him.

"Oh, yes, so sorry!" He hastily rolled off her and stumbled to his feet, brushing off leaves and dirt before he bent to offer the young lady assistance.

"My apologies, miss. I was not looking where I was going." He still couldn't see her in the dim light, but her voice was soft and husky. It made him think of bare skin, satin sheets, and soft sighs of pleasure. His body instantly reacted with arousal, and his muscles tensed.

"The fault was entirely mine." The young lady rose with his aid, her gloved hands warm in his. They moved away from the shadow of the tall hedges and into a shaft of light from the lamps near the entrance leading back into the assembly hall.

The lamplight illuminated a well-formed body draped in white muslin, violets embroidered at the waist and hem. The lady herself was no great beauty by patrician standards, at least not at first glance—her nose was too pert, her chin a tad too pointed. But when he studied her face more closely, he found her features strangely fit together and she was in fact very pretty. Her blue eyes were almond-shaped rather than round pools of color. The tilt of her eyes and the languorous half-lidded gaze that seemed natural to her was dreamy, and thick sooty lashes framed them, making the blue brighter. Like staring at fresh cornflowers. It made Ambrose think of naked bodies writhing in passion amid garden blooms. As she continued to gaze softly back at him, her lips parted, and he knew that whoever bedded this woman would stare into her eyes and make love as though in a dream. He shook his head, clearing the haze of curiosity and desire.

"I see I am not the only one escaping the horde inside," she teased him. Her lips curved slightly when she spoke, as though smiling came naturally to her. It made her far prettier than he'd originally thought.

Ambrose wanted to smile himself, something he hadn't done in years. A smirk when possible, a grin where needed, or a leer when necessary—but a genuine smile was rare for him.

"I couldn't stand another minute in there," he confessed. For a moment he forgot about the wager. It was obvious he wouldn't find Rockford's daughter at the dance tonight. He would have met her in the earlier introductions when he'd first arrived. He could take a moment to enjoy this woman and her company before facing the crowds inside. Would she stay out here with him and continue talking? Or would she seek shelter inside and avoid him like any smart young lady would do?

She raised a lace fan and wafted it close to her cheeks, which were a little too rosy. "I don't blame you. I can't stand the heat when everyone starts dancing. I came outside to cool off." The young lady backed up a step, not exactly a retreat, but Ambrose acted out of primal instinct and mirrored her movement by stepping toward her.

Perhaps tonight wouldn't be a total waste of his time. He could steal a few kisses from a few ladies until he found his quarry for the bet. It wouldn't do him any harm to enjoy a few minutes with this enchanting creature.

"As there is no one to introduce us, might I have the honor of claiming your name?" Ambrose leaned one shoulder casually on the stone wall in front of her, effectively blocking her entrance back into the ballroom. Gardens were *always* preferred for stolen kisses.

"And allow you to create scandal?" The woman tried to sound imperious and scandalized, but she broke down into an adorable fit of giggles.

Normally Ambrose hated the twittering sound of giggles, but this was entirely different.

"Very well, let's be scandalous then." She rewarded him with a smile that hit him right behind the knees.

True mirth and humor shone in her eyes, and against his better judgment he barked out a laugh. It felt...good.

He'd become so jaded in recent years, he hadn't laughed much either.

"I'm Alexandra."

"Do people call you Alex, then?"

"No." A glint of merriment sparked in her eyes, but she raised one brow in challenge. He could tell she was lying about that, and she was teasing him, too.

"May I?" Ambrose pushed away from the wall and straightened to his full height, moving one step closer.

"You wish to call me Alex?" She leaned into him the faintest bit, her eyes half-closed as she stared at his mouth. What an easy prize she would be, but well worth the conquest tonight.

"Yes," he murmured and cupped her chin. His thumb traced the cupid's bow of her lips, pulled them apart a little. Her shallow, panting breaths warmed his thumb and heated his blood. His cock hardened painfully in his buckskin trousers.

"And what should I call you?" Her lips moved in a luscious dance as she spoke.

He was momentarily lost in visions of stealing kisses and pinning her to the wall, showing her all the wicked delights of what his hands and mouth could do while the muted sounds from the ballroom drowned her out her moans of pleasure. It was a skill he'd perfected over the years, one that made him dangerous at any dance where young ladies were left unattended by their chaperones or mamas.

"My friends call me Ambrose."

"Oh?" Her nose wrinkled adorably, and he could tell she was trying to stave off another attack of giggles. "Is that your way of telling me we are friends?"

He chuckled. "No, but I would certainly like to be. My full name is Ambrose Worthing."

The haze of desire vanished in between heartbeats. "Worthing!" She pulled back, trepidation and recognition flashing across her face.

"You've heard of me then?" So his reputation had reached at least one person in Lothbrook. Perhaps this small hamlet of a village wasn't as remote as he'd believed. Until she'd reacted, he'd begun to think he wasn't wicked enough for his name to stretch past the outskirts of London.

"Yes, I have heard of you. Your reputation precedes you."

"Oh? And what reputation is that?" He couldn't help but want to know if she'd say it. She'd been so bold before. Would she cease to be so charming and fascinating when she was faced with a rakehell of the first order straight from the gambling hells in London?

"You are a rake," Alex announced in an accusatory voice that made him smile.

"Yes. What of it?" Damned, he couldn't keep from smiling. Her eyes had widened, and she licked her lips nervously. She knew what being a rake actually meant... and not just to her reputation.

"I can't be seen with you out here. Not *alone*." Alex retreated, but Ambrose was too fascinated to let her escape. He was not a villain and would never force a woman to do anything she didn't wish, but damned if he wouldn't stay her long enough to steal a kiss.

When she'd assumed he was just another gentleman, she'd let him touch her lips, lean in close enough for a kiss, but now she was fleeing all because of one little word...*rake*. He couldn't resist the chase now that it had begun.

"Alex, love, where do you think you're going?" He caged her between his arms and the wall. She bumped into the bricks behind her, and her chin lifted as she met him with a defiant stare.

"Let me go back inside." There was steel beneath that sensual tone, and he couldn't help but admire her for that. Not such a wilting wallflower then.

"What has you so frightened? One minute we were having a polite conversation, and the next you're fleeing simply because I told you my name."

She arched a brow. "We were having a polite conversation until I learned that you were the sort of man who could ruin me by the simple act of being alone with you. Now if you'll kindly let me pass..."

Ambrose smiled, pinning her with the weight of his seductive snare. "'Tis a pity you fear passion."

Alex scoffed, completely unimpressed by a look he'd used to break many hearts and quite a few beds.

"Did you think that would work? Challenge me to stay and let you compromise me in the name of conquering my fears? I'm not some country peahen." She shoved hard at his chest, her determination making her even more alluring.

Ambrose slid an arm around her waist, pulling her against him. "I would never say you were a peahen. You remind me more of a doe. Deep, expressive eyes, sleek limbs. All you need is a proper buck, one to mount you and claim you as his with deep, powerful thrusts." He painted the verbal picture and punctuated it with a slow roll of his pelvis against hers.

A flush of red stained her cheeks, her lips parting in shock. He'd probably gone too far, but he took a strange delight in provoking this woman.

"Would you like that, Alex? Do you want a man to *possess* you, take you hard until you scream?" His provocative words had the desired effect.

She blinked at him, desire battling outrage in her eyes. Alex was a woman who craved passion but knew wanting it was dangerous. Smart girl.

"You know what I want?" she demanded breathlessly.

"Yes?" He pressed fully against her, his body ready to take hers. It would be so easy to lift her skirts, wrap her lovely legs around his hips, and take her here. He could silence her cries with his lips. God, he wanted that more than he'd wanted anything in a long damned time.

"I want you to get out of my way." He sensed the

movement too late to stop her, and he felt the agonizing pain slice through him as her knee jutted up, a slither of silks and satins, and rammed into him, crushing his bollocks and crippling him. His throat closed with panic, and he clutched his crotch, his ability to breathe escaping him as stars danced before his eyes.

"Christ!" he hissed.

In his agony he barely noticed her leaving, a whisper of her dress as she pushed past him and back into the ball-room, leaving him broken and alone, holding on to the aching cock he had a moment before been pressing against her. He rested one palm against the brick wall, gasping and trying to control the surge of shooting pain from his balls up to his chest.

Bloody hell, the woman had one hell of a leg.

When the pain at last subsided, he started laughing. Alex was one hell of a woman, and he couldn't wait to get her in his bed. He would worry about the Earl of Rock-ford's daughter tomorrow. Tonight he would play buck to Alex's doe.

2

"Heavens, I can't believe I did that." Alexandra covered her mouth to stifle a laugh. She hid at the back of the assembly room with her best friend, Perdita Darby. Her heart was pounding, and her body was trembling. Thankfully, the music drowned out the sound of their laughter. The moment she'd rushed inside she'd sought out her friend, and they'd ducked behind a wall of impressive matrons who were watching the dancing with critical eyes to see which young men might suit their daughters.

"You truly kicked a man between his legs?" Perdita seemed torn between laughing and gasping in scandalized shock. This was why she loved her friend. They were both a bit of outcasts in Lothbrook because neither one of them was inclined to marry, and the thought of kneeing a man's bollocks made them both laugh.

Lord, we are doomed to be spinsters, but at least we shall be together, Alex thought, laughing still.

"I did! I don't know what came over me, but there he was, talking about...possessing me, and I just...kicked!" Alex blushed and covered her face in her hands for a minute to collect herself. If anyone found out she'd behaved like such a hoyden, she'd be in real trouble. She was relieved her mother had given up on marrying her off and had gone to London on her own for the season. If she'd been here and seen what Alex had been up to...

I'd never hear the end of it.

"If he was trying to kiss you, it was only fitting that you put a stop to his forward behavior. You can't afford to be compromised by a man like Ambrose Worthing, even if he is the *finest* man ever to be seen. Although, one kiss might have been worth it..." Perdita replied in all seriousness, but her lips twitched as she mentioned a kiss.

"Perdita!" Alex gasped in a hushed whisper. "You wouldn't actually kiss a rake like him, would you?" Perdita's statement shocked her. Was her friend actually considering going about kissing rakes? Surely not sensible, sweet Perdita. Between the two of them, Perdita was far more adept at navigating social situations, but that probably had something to do with her mother constantly throwing parties, balls, and picnics in an attempt to entice gentlemen to court Perdita. Alex was more of a hoyden than anything else—she'd readily admit to that. It was far better to be racing about the country on her horse than to be stuck inside like most other ladies her age.

"Of course I *would*. Aren't you the least bit curious as to what it would be like, kissing a man like that? One who actually knows what to do with a woman?" Perdita's dark-brown hair was pulled up, but loose curls teased the slope of her neck, and when she glanced about the curls danced on her skin. "You know what they say about him in London..."

"You mean about how he..." Alex's words died on her tongue as Ambrose strode straight toward her. Fury black-ened his eyes, but a sensual smile hovered at the edge of his perfectly curved lips as though he'd already planned his revenge. Whatever he'd dreamed up, she knew it wouldn't be good.

"Oh dear, Perdy, save me quick!" Alex shoved her friend in front of her just as Ambrose reached them.

"Mr. Worthing, I presume?" Perdita flashed him a charming smile. She wasn't a diamond of the first water, but men seemed to enjoy spending time with her during social engagements. There was a liveliness and playfulness to her that made her instantly amiable. It was a rare man who didn't enjoy being around Perdita when she was playing the part of a charming young lady. Ambrose, however, seemed unaffected.

"Yes. You must be Miss Darby. I've had the pleasure of meeting your mother."

Even though his reply was directed at Perdita, his gaze

scorched a path up and down Alex's body, despite the human shield her friend presented.

Perdita chuckled wryly. "I doubt my mother's acquaintance was much of a pleasure, but you are kind to say so. Are you staying in Lothbrook long?" She was a master conversationalist and wasn't at all perturbed at being used as a shield. Alex was never more thankful Perdita was her friend.

Perdita suddenly nudged backward with her elbow, prodding Alex to try to slip away from her and Ambrose. A wonderful idea...a quick escape...

Ambrose, under the apparent guise of avoiding a nearby dancing couple, stepped closer to them and blocked Alex's route to freedom. "I'm staying at the inn, but I've received an invitation to join the Earl of Rockford at his estate."

Alex's blood drained from her face. Her father had invited one of London's most notorious rakehells to stay in their home? What on earth could he be thinking? Surely he wouldn't have done so if he'd known of Ambrose's reputation.

"You are acquainted with my father?" she blurted out.

"Your father?" His responding look of confusion caught her off guard. He didn't know who she was.

"Yes, James Westfall, the Earl of Rockford."

This time it was Ambrose who paled. "You're Rockford's daughter?" An unreadable expression filled his rich brown eyes. Earlier in the darkened garden, she hadn't been able to make out his features as clearly, only that he'd been a tall, muscled man with a smooth voice and a decent face. But now in the light of the assembly room, when she was really having to face him, she couldn't help but hate him just a little. He was too good-looking. With dark hair and dark eyes, full lips that seemed most comfortable when curled in a slightly sardonic grin, and a strong chin and straight nose, he was an ideal specimen of a man. Just like Marshall had been...

She shoved thoughts of Marshall away. The last thing she wanted to do was think of the young man who'd broken her heart five years ago before he'd left for London.

She forced herself to eye Ambrose critically. She liked being able to read a person, and it unsettled her, not having a clue what he was thinking. She shifted restlessly on her feet. If Alex didn't know better, she'd have thought the look was that of quickly masked calculation.

"Mr. Worthing is acquainted with your father?" Perdita looked between them, amusement tugging the corners of her lips.

Ambrose recovered himself and smiled warmly. "I met him when I was a lad. Our fathers are old friends. I've only recently had the opportunity to renew the acquaintance."

"Oh," Alex breathed in relief. "You won't be staying long then."

"Alex!" Perdita jabbed her elbow sharply in Alex's ribs.

"*Oomf!*" Alex hissed from the discomfort of that unexpected little blow and glared at her friend.

"Alex? You told me no one calls you that." Ambrose crossed his arms, and Alex couldn't help but admire the fine cut of his dark blue waistcoat. With broad shoulders, narrow hips, and muscled legs in buckskin breeches, Ambrose Worthing was a vision of masculine perfection. It was a pity he was no better than a bounder who preyed upon ladies of quality by seducing them for his own pleasures. A man like him should have had a sweet disposition and a kind heart and be loyal to a wonderful wife. But alas, the most attractive men were always the most dangerous, the rakes, the rogues—devils each and every last one.

"Her friends call her Alex." Perdita flipped her fan open and looked at Alex from behind the lacy contraption, hiding a wide grin.

"Well then, Alex, I am delighted to make your acquaintance and am quite sure I shall win you as a friend." Ambrose captured her hand and bent to press a kiss on the inside of her wrist. Alex's blood heated at the hot pressure of his lips. He flicked his tongue against her pulse. She jerked her hand back in surprise. She'd suffered a hundred kisses to the hand over the last few years, and none had such an effect as Ambrose's.

Why would he be different? It is probably because he infuriates me so, with his arrogance and his determination to woo. Well, I shall not be wooed.

"Miss Darby." Ambrose kissed Perdita's hand in a much more gentlemanly fashion. "Would you care to dance?" He flashed a smile in her direction, ignoring Alex completely.

Perdita's face fell. "I'm so sorry, Mr. Worthing. My dance card is full. Alex, however, has the next waltz free."

"They allow you to waltz here?" Ambrose's brows drew together in puzzlement.

"Alex can. Her father convinced the matrons of Lothbrook to allow it." Perdita announced this with a great deal of pride. After all, it had been after the request her father had made, and it had taken Alex's best behavior for two seasons to prove to the matrons she could be trusted to dance the scandalous waltz.

"Dancing on the edge of scandal?" Ambrose quirked his lips, reading her silent thoughts.

"I'm twenty-two, Mr. Worthing. Even though I am unmarried, I should be able to waltz. My father and the matrons agree. It helps that my reputation is beyond reproach."

"Not for long," Ambrose muttered.

"I beg your pardon?" she demanded.

"Shall we dance then?" Ambrose stepped around Perdita and once more claimed her hand, pulling her toward the dancers lining up for the waltz.

He tugged her into his arms, fitting her body snugly against his.

"Move back, Mr. Worthing, you're too close," Alex protested. Flashes of heat scoured her body in tiny flames, licking at her breasts and between her legs. Being flush against him nearly robbed her of her senses. She'd danced other waltzes, but no man had affected her like this. Alex didn't like it.

"That is the point of dancing a waltz, Alex. A man likes to hold his woman close, feel her breasts against his chest. He wants to feel her body against the length of his."

"But I'm not *your* woman," Alex pointed out. If she had her way, she'd never belong to any man. She was quite content to live the rest of her days alone and in control of her own destiny. Her father allowed her quite a bit of freedom, and someday she would have the lands and money settled upon her in a trust that her uncle would be in control of, but her uncle was a dear old man and would let her go on as she pleased. There was no need to marry. After what she'd suffered when Marshall had left Lothbrook, she couldn't bear to think of falling in love with another man, and she certainly wouldn't marry someone unless she loved him.

"But you could be my woman. All you need say is 'Please, Ambrose,' and I'm yours to command. I only wish to worship at the altar of such loveliness." His tone was rich and low, teasing, and yet not mocking as she'd expected.

Alex scoffed, trying to ignore the way his bewitching voice made her feel. "Do those pretty phrases actually work? Do women fall at your feet begging for your attentions?"

"Every single time," he assured her with a brazen smile

as the dance started.

Very well, I can play too. She flashed him a smile back.

Alex aimed purposely for his foot and trod on it. He narrowed his eyes but gave no other indication that he'd noticed. His fingers around her waist dug deep. She stifled a gasp when the primal possessive touch shot straight to her core, making her wet. That was a problem.

She was not a stranger to sexual desire. She'd come upon one of her father's grooms once in the summer when he'd been cleaning the stables out. He had removed his waistcoat and shirt as he mucked out the stalls. Alex had leaned against the door, hidden from view as she'd watched the play of light and shadows on his muscled body. That was the first time her body had awakened, but she had not acted on that desire. And much later, when she'd fallen in love with Marshall, they had stolen kisses in the shadows of the stable and behind the hedges of her garden and it had been wonderful. The dizzying feel of building desire had left her aching and desperate to know fulfillment. But she'd never gone past kisses. She would not let a man like Ambrose draw her in with honeyed words or heated gazes. It reminded her too much of Marshall, and thoughts of him always sliced her deep.

A little voice inside her head whispered that Ambrose wasn't Marshall.

She didn't want to want Ambrose. She couldn't afford to give in to hunger for a man like him. He'd ruin her and not look back once his coach left Lothbrook. Alex raised her eyes to his face. His aquiline nose and sculpted jaw were beautiful. The temptation to be seduced was impossibly strong, but she would not give in.

Lucky for me, his arrogance makes him less attractive.

"You know, I would never bed a man like you. You're an arrogant, pompous arse."

For a second he blinked, as though startled by her tart response. Then he recovered and smiled. "You don't know the first thing about arses, my dear."

She flinched at the fierce, leonine look in his eyes.

"I sense you don't like me, but I wonder if it's men in general, dear Alex, that sends you into a such a state of scorn?" he mused thoughtfully. When she didn't respond, he continued. "Did you love another man? Is that it? Someone broke your heart?" He was teasing, but she stumbled at his too accurate guess.

"Please, I don't wish to dance anymore," she whispered, trying to get him to stop. She didn't want to talk about Marshall, didn't want to think about him or the dreams she'd built that had been shattered when he abandoned her to marry another woman for more money.

Ambrose stared at her, and she looked away, not wishing to see a look of gleeful pride.

"I hadn't—I'm sorry...I didn't realize I might be right. I was jesting. Please, Alex, let us finish the dance." His tone was gentle, and it drew her face back to his. Those brown eyes were warm and soft and apologetic.

They continued the waltz in silence, the music

cloaking them in its rhythmic pulse. Alex and Ambrose fell into a relaxed pace, legs perfectly in sync, bodies just the right distance apart. He was a wonderful dancer, she would allow him that.

"What are you thinking about?" he asked when they reached the corner of the room and began to move back out amid the twirling couples.

"Hmm?" Alex was barely listening. She was caught up in the lovely feel of dancing with him.

"You look both relaxed and perplexed all at once."

"Oh. I was thinking that you are a wonderful dancer. Most of the men in Lothbrook have trod on my toes too often for me to enjoy dancing. Until now." Even Marshall hadn't been a good dancer. Passable, yes, but never divine like this. She'd always wanted to waltz with a man who could do it properly, and now she was glad to find that desire hadn't been a waste. This was more than agreeable —it was lovely. Almost too lovely, and she knew it would come to an end.

"So you admit I'm not *all* bad." Ambrose's smile was piratical. It was possessive, predatory, and completely intoxicating. The power of it impacted her deep inside, like an explosion of sensation and hunger.

This is why rakes are so dangerous. Women would do anything to win a smile like that.

"You are still *mostly* bad," she replied, but it was impossible not to laugh a little as she said it.

Ambrose laughed too. "I'll accept *mostly bad* as a credit

to my irresistible charm."

"I suppose that next you'll tell me reformed rakes make the best husbands."

"Lord no, but I'd love for you to try to reform me." He pulled her an inch closer and lowered his gaze to her lips. "Perhaps we could discuss the ways in which my wickedness could be handled. You could tie me down and torture me with that sweet little mou...Ack!" Ambrose gasped as Alex purposely stomped on his feet again.

"Hellfire! You bloodthirsty wench," he growled and pulled her hard into him just as the music faded and the dancing couples split apart.

"Let go of me," Alex hissed. If someone noticed them, it could ruin her, especially given how close he was holding her and the fact that one of his hands cupped her bottom. It felt good—too good—and she didn't like that either.

Ambrose hesitated a moment too long before he moved back and dropped into a courtly bow.

"Alex, thank you for the lovely dance. I believe I shall see you soon. Perhaps later this evening."

"Why?" she demanded. Her tone was more breathless than she would have liked.

"I must return to the inn and have my things delivered to your father's estate. His invitation to remain a fortnight as his guest is too kind. I wouldn't want to insult him."

Oh no, she was not about to let a rake like him sleep under the same roof.

"He won't let you step one foot in our house. Not after

I tell him what you said to me."

Ambrose's laugh was soft and dark. "I wouldn't do that, Alex. I might just tell him how well acquainted we are. He'll insist I do the proper thing, and I shall of course."

"The proper thing?" Alex wasn't following any of this.

"Warn you father against me, and I'll tell him I tossed your skirts up and claimed you as mine this very night. Then you'll find you're stuck with me as a husband."

Alex's jaw scraped the floor. "Why would you do that? You don't want to marry me. You don't even *know* me."

"No, I don't know you. But marriages have started on less. I know you don't wish to marry me either. So we shall endeavor to keep our mouths shut, unless of course you wish to do other things with those lips than speak."

She weighed his words, trying to find a way around his threat of telling her father she'd been ruined. Even though it wouldn't be true, her father would be inclined to believe Ambrose as a gentleman. And he seemed like just the sort of man who would marry her to get revenge.

"You're the wickedest man I've ever met," Alex ground out, planting a fake smile on her face. He had won that small battle, but she was determined to win the war. She was going to make sure his stay at her home was less than agreeable, so much so that he'd run screaming back to London.

"Why, thank you." He brushed his lips over her knuckles and vanished into the crowd.

Alex stepped out of the carriage, her feet aching from all the dancing she'd done tonight. She was looking forward to a hot bath and a warm fire before bed as well as her after-ball dessert left out by the cook. No matter how she tried to direct her thoughts as she walked toward her home, her mind kept straying back to one forbidden subject: Ambrose Worthing, the notorious rakehell from London.

After her encounter with Ambrose and that waltz, he'd departed from the assembly hall, which had left her feeling safe and yet strangely disappointed. She didn't want to admit it, but she'd longed to have one more dance with him, even though she had decided she didn't like him. He was a marvelous dancer.

Her father, James Westfall, the Earl of Rockford, greeted her at the door.

"Papa, what are you doing awake at this hour! It's close to midnight. You ought to be in bed." She hugged him, noticing his bright smile and feeling a sense of unease creep through her. A footman removed her cloak as she stepped into the house.

"We have a guest! I forgot to mention it this morning when you were here, but I've invited the son of an old friend to come and stay for a few weeks."

"But—"

"There's no need to fret. A room's been prepared for him, and it's all settled with the cook for our meals. Rest assured, I have handled everything." Her father declared this proudly and then turned to the drawing room door that was ajar. "Worthing, come and meet my daughter, Alexandra!" he called out.

Worthing? No...no...no... Surely this was a nightmare. She'd hoped to have a few more hours of solace before he arrived. Alex glared at Ambrose as he appeared in the drawing room door and flashed her a wicked, knowing grin.

"Alex, this is Mr. Ambrose Worthing."

"A pleasure," Ambrose said as he took her hand and lifted it to his lips, kissing the backs of her fingers.

She frowned at him, which thankfully went unnoticed by her father.

"Why don't we all sit by the fire for a minute before going up to bed? I'd like for you both to get properly acquainted," her father suggested happily as he led her and Ambrose back into the drawing room.

Alex didn't immediately follow. She stood there, rooted to the spot, her mind racing frantically. What if he told her father she'd kicked him in the groin? What if her father guessed he had tried to kiss her? What if—

"Are you coming, Lady Alexandra?" Ambrose asked, leaning one shoulder against the doorway, forcing her to come face-to-face with him if she wished to get inside the room. She approached hesitantly and then stopped inches from him.

"Ahem," she coughed politely, and with a cheeky grin, he stepped back, letting her brush past him so she could take a seat by the fire.

The fire crackled and popped, shooting sparks to the edges of the fireplace. Alex warmed her hands over the flames before sitting down.

"Thank you again for the invitation, my lord. It has been years since I've been here." Ambrose took a seat, his muscled frame lounging back into a winged chair. A smug grin curved his lips when she dared to glance at him. Anger sparked beneath her skin, and a flush of embarrassment came when she remembered that kiss. How dare he come in here, smiling like that...in her house! She struggled to compose herself.

I can handle this. I can deal with him.

So he thought he could make himself comfortable

here? She bit her lip to keep from laughing. He wouldn't be for long. She'd see to that.

"It has been an age, hasn't it? Since before you left for Eton. Alex was still a babe in the nursery when you two came down for fishing." Her father's face had softened as he spoke, and a wistfulness made his eyes gleam.

Alex hadn't thought her father was lonely—both he and Alex weren't much for social gatherings—but perhaps he did wish to see his friends more. She visited Perdita often, but her father didn't leave the house much except when she convinced him. He preferred his books in his study and going hunting or fishing, but those activities were best enjoyed when he was with companions.

The old resentment at her mother—who spent half the year in London and when home was always busy—rose up in Alex as the thought of her father's loneliness took off. She knew her parents weren't a love match, but a political one. The alignment of two strong English families had been more important than marrying for passion. Alex had grown up all too aware of that fact. It wasn't that they didn't care for each other. They did love each other in their own way. But there was little passion in that love.

"How is your father, Ambrose? Last he was here was before Christmas of the previous year." Her father set his spectacles aside on the small reading table near him and leaned closer to their guest.

"He is quite well. He and my mother are staying with friends in Edinburgh for the Little Season."

"Are they? Good for them. But you must tell him to come down here and hunt with me in the fall. Shooting has been excellent these last few years. You should come too, if you're not otherwise engaged."

Alex chose that moment to cut in. "Papa, I'm sure Mr. Worthing has much better things to do than come down here to shoot."

Her father harrumphed. "Nonsense, dear, men like to shoot things. Don't they, Worthing?"

"Indeed." Ambrose winked at Alex, making her shake with rage. "A man loves to hunt all sorts of things." His eyes seemed to tell her what his lips did not. *Like pheasant, foxes, and...women.*

"Excellent! We shall invite you down then this fall." Her father suddenly sat up. "Goodness, I haven't even properly introduced you to my darling girl, have I?"

Alex sighed. This was why her mother didn't bring her father to London. He had no head for society's expectations of introductions and formalities.

"I did indeed have the pleasure of meeting her and dancing with her at the assembly rooms tonight." Ambrose smiled.

"Ah, good, good." Her father was still blushing. "Alex, dear, would you pour us some glasses of brandy?" He nodded at the decanter, which sat on a table at the back of the room.

"Of course, Papa." She shot an unamused look at Ambrose and then got up to pour the gentlemen glasses.

LAUREN SMITH

"How is the Countess of Rockford?" Ambrose was behaving like a perfect gentleman. There was not one hint of impropriety, not one glint of lust in his eyes as he conversed with her father like an old friend.

"Irene is well. She too is off visiting people. She's in London with her sister for the next month. Alex and I are quite beside ourselves with boredom, aren't we, dear?" Her father was teasing of course.

At this, Alex couldn't resist laughing. They were both glad to be left alone in Lothbrook.

They'd been excited at the prospect of a quiet home for a month. Her mother loved to entertain and attend every social engagement that came her way. But Alex and her father found it exhausting.

"We're delighted you came to visit us. Aren't we, Alex?" her father prompted cheerily.

"Yes," Alex replied coolly. Her father didn't notice her tone. Ambrose did. She could swear his lips quirked the slightest bit. Had he ever really smiled, one that wasn't intended to seduce? Each time his eyes flicked to her, those sensual lips quirked. And each time, she was drawn to those lips, watching them, even though she hated herself for it.

"Well, the hour is late. You two have been dancing the night away. No doubt you both wish to be tucked into bed. Come, Worthing, I'll have a footman escort you to your room."

The second her father's back was turned, Ambrose

34

licked his lips, eyeing her the way a cat did a fat canary. Alex flushed. It was imperative she get out of this room and to the safety of her chambers after she'd had a chance to set some of her plans in motion.

"Goodnight, Papa, Mr. Worthing." She kissed her father's cheek, and without looking back at Ambrose, she left.

She rushed down to the kitchen. The large kitchen was carefully swept, pots hanging from the wooden rack over the primary preparation counter. Spices hung from twine near the windows, scenting the room with basil and rosemary. She found the cook, Mrs. Cooper, taking stock of the inventory in the larders.

"Eggs, flour...salt, and lemons. I want to make a meringue in a few days."

The scullery maid, Beth, had a paper with a pencil and was jotting down notes of what they needed. Alex smiled. If there was one thing about her father that she loved more than anything, it was that he insisted his staff be educated in reading and writing—not just the upper staff, but the lower staff right down to the scullery maid.

Beth pursed her lips as she scribbled down "Lemons." Then she glanced up and saw Alex, and with a startled but shy smile, she nudged the cook in the back.

"What is it, girl?" Mrs. Cooper turned around and brushed back a lock of dark hair that had fallen out of her cap. "Oh, Lady Alex, what can I do for you?"

Feeling a tad guilty but determined not to change her

mind, she approached the cook. "Mrs. Cooper, our guest, Mr. Worthing, has very particular appetites."

"Oh, aye? What does he like? You know me, my lady. I can fix anything." Mrs. Cooper looked proud.

"That's just it—he prefers porridge for breakfast and luncheon. And he wishes to be served in his room at six o'clock in the morning on a tray. He doesn't like to dine with the others."

"Porridge? Surely..." Mrs. Cooper frowned and scratched at her head.

"Yes," Alex said. "And don't sweeten it with any sugar or fruit. He prefers it bitter, with some extra salt."

Beth made a sour face at the description, and Alex couldn't blame her. Porridge was bad enough, but salty porridge—well, that was quite another horror on its own.

"Are you quite sure, my lady? I'd be happy to prepare some nice eggs and—"

"Just the porridge, Mrs. Cooper." She had to bite her lip to keep from laughing at what poor Ambrose would do when he had to eat salty porridge tomorrow morning.

"Very well," Mrs. Cooper sighed. It wasn't in her nature to prepare anything distasteful. She took pride in her culinary abilities.

"Oh, and can you tell Mrs. Marsden that we'll need a footman to act as Mr. Worthing's valet tonight. His own valet will be coming down from London tomorrow."

"Of course." Mrs. Cooper nodded and bustled off toward Mrs. Marsden's office. The housekeeper would know which of the young men would be most suited as a temporary valet. Alex would let him have that at least. She grinned and had to keep from rubbing her hands together in glee. If he insisted on testing her, she was going to see that other things would go awry while he was here.

Really, I ought to be ashamed of myself. But I'm not.

Alex went back upstairs to her own bedchamber. Her lady's maid, Mary, was tidying up her vanity table, and she smiled when Alex walked in.

"Evening, my lady." A dimple formed in Mary's cheek when she smiled.

"Evening, Mary." She closed the bedroom door and then turned her back to let her maid loosen the laces of her gown and then her stays.

"I take it the ball was exciting?" Mary asked, her tone full of hope. Alex always shared with her the details of the events she went to, since Mary seemed to enjoy the tales of the wild hunts young ladies went on for husbands.

"It was, but only because I ran into the infamous Mr. Worthing."

Mary gasped. "Isn't he the guest who just arrived tonight?"

Alex let the ball gown drop to the floor, and she stepped out of it and then shimmied out of her loosened stays before slipping out of her shoes.

"Yes, but you remember I told you about him, one of London's infamous rakes?" She lifted her foot onto the bed and unfastened her garters before peeling her stockings off one foot and then the other.

Mary retrieved the gown and stays from the floor, draping them over the back of a chair while she collected the stockings.

"I remember." Her maid's green eyes were large. "And he's staying here?" This was added with a scandalized whisper. "Does his lordship not know of Mr. Worthing's reputation?"

Alex shook her head. "Papa doesn't listen to idle London gossip, and he certainly wouldn't trust it over his own feelings. He and Mr. Worthing's father are good friends. So be careful around him, Mary. Rakes have roving eyes and wandering hands." She didn't honestly think he'd attempt to seduce a lady's maid, but she wanted Mary on her guard all the same.

"Don't worry about me, my lady. I have two brothers. There's not a man alive who can catch me unawares." Mary giggled as she said this and picked up the white nightgown from the bed and helped Alex into it.

A breeze outside the window suddenly dragged the branches along the glass in a screeching sound, making both girls jump.

"Mrs. Cooper told us over supper it will likely storm tonight," Mary said.

Alex had to agree. The scent of rain had hung heavy in the air when she left the dance. She picked up her dark-blue dressing gown and slipped it on before approaching the window and peering out into the night. The garden below began to mist as the clouds let a sweeping rain move through. The drops splattered against the window.

"Will you be needing anything else, my lady?" Mary asked as she collected Alex's clothes.

"No, thank you."

Alex watched the rain continue to roll in heavy waves across the garden and tried to forget how it had felt to waltz with Ambrose. It was a terrible thing to have a wonderful memory like that creep up on her over and over ever since she'd departed the assembly rooms. But she simply couldn't banish it from her mind.

I should not be tempted by him.

No matter what she told herself, she *was* tempted. It was a good thing she despised everything else about the man. She would not give in to such an arrogant, pompous arse.

Lost in thoughts of scaring him out of her house with bad porridge, she was startled when her stomach growled. She should have nipped something from the kitchens when she'd been down there earlier.

Might as well go back down. Mrs. Cooper always left her a delicious tart after balls. And she wouldn't sleep well tonight; the sound of the rain always made her restless. She'd ride out the storm and feast on something sweet.

And she would not think any more about waltzing with a rake.

4

Bloody hell. I'm attracted to the little minx.

Ambrose paced inside his bedchamber, mulling over the night's strange turn of events.

Alex was an intriguing creature. Wit, ferocity, and repressed desire, all bottled up in a body he ached to hold in his arms. Hell, he wanted to do more than hold her, but he doubted he'd get far tonight. But he certainly had every intention of fulfilling his end of the wager and seducing her.

Once he realized who she was, the bet had seemed less important than his genuine desire to take her to bed. Part of him knew he was damned because once he'd fulfilled his bet, he wouldn't be welcomed back into this house by her or her father. They would never know he'd sought to save her from a fate with a worse man than him.

He buried the guilt deep inside, a talent he'd mastered

over the years when he'd indulged in his wicked ways with the ladies of the *ton*. Rather than wallow in thoughts of burning bridges with a man who was like a second father to him, he turned his thoughts to Alex and her delightfully conflicting personality.

Who knew that Rockford had such an enchanting daughter? He'd come here often as a lad before leaving for school, but he'd never noticed her. She'd been tucked away in the nursery, six years his junior. As a younger man he'd never paid attention to the earl's private life.

He'd been surprised to discover that Rockford had a daughter when he'd heard Langley boasting about the wager he'd put in White's betting book. It had been out of duty to his father's friend and an intent to prevent the young lady the most harm by making her seduction quick and painless. But now that he was here and had seen her, spoken to her, Ambrose wanted to make her seduction long and pleasurable. He could spend months slowly turning her ire against him into irresistible sexual hunger.

He knew he shouldn't be enjoying the earl's hospitality when his plan was to pluck the daughter's virginity like a ripe apricot. An apricot whose sweet juices would taste like nectar when he buried his head between her thighs. He might be a cad, but still better him than the other men at the club who'd wished to take on the wager. Ambrose's former friend, Vaughn, now Viscount Darlington, had been debating on whether to sign his name to the betting book.

A shudder racked Ambrose at the thought. A spitfire like Alex would not last long in bed with a man like Vaughn. Vaughn liked his bedplay on the rough side. He didn't hurt women, but the need to dominate was always present, and gentle-bred ladies like Alex might be frightened. Ambrose didn't have the same needs as his friend. Every now and then he liked to tie a woman up so he could torture her with slow kisses and touches in ways she'd be too shy to allow otherwise. For some women, taking control away from them helped them relax and enjoy passion.

A woman like Alex with a defiant streak was not a woman who should be tamed. She should be seduced into wild wantonness. Alex would be a wonderfully sensual creature, and the man to open her eyes would be richly rewarded.

There was a soft knock on his door.

"Come in," he replied.

A young lad of eighteen or nineteen entered; his clothing identifying him as a footman.

"Good evening, Mr. Worthing. My name is Ben. The lady of the house sent me to see to you as your valet while you are here."

"Thank you, Ben." He smiled at the lad, who set about unpacking his valise.

Toeing off his boots, Ambrose leaned against his bed and started on the buttons of his waistcoat. Ben helped retrieve his clothes as he removed them piece by piece.

When he was down to breeches and a white lawn shirt, he raked a hand through his hair and focused on tomorrow. Mrs. Darby had invited him to her annual picnic by sending him an invitation when he'd had to pass her on the way out of the assembly hall, and he knew Alex was going because she and the Darby girl, Perdita, were friends. Ambrose's lips curved up into a smile, one of delicious wickedness. Picnics were excellent for seductions. It was impossibly easy to get a woman behind a hedge or a tree and have his way with her. The fact that they could be discovered at any moment only heightened the intensity of their release.

Ben held out his knee-length silk damask banyan, and Ambrose slid it on. It fit close to his body. He left his trousers on for the moment; he waited to remove those until he was certain he was going to bed.

"Thank you, Ben. That will be all for this evening."

"Good night, Mr. Worthing." The young man slipped out into the hall and closed the door, leaving Ambrose alone with his thoughts.

Ambrose was in the middle of debating whether to go to bed when he heard the soft click of a door open down the hall. Intrigued, he put his ear to the door, listening to bare feet padding past his door. The footfalls were distinctly feminine. Ambrose grinned. Servants wouldn't be barefoot, but the daughter of the Earl of Rockford might.

"Let it never be said I skipped such a perfect opportunity." He chuckled and eased his door open.

The billowing shape of Alex's nightgown partially covered by a dressing gown was a beacon in the dark hall. Her hair was unbound, the long locks flowing down to the middle of her back, the ends slightly curled. As she tiptoed down the hall, her ankles drew his attention like no other ankles had. They weren't tiny or delicate, but they were seductive. He wanted them to lock around his waist or link around his calves as he pounded into her, making her writhe in pleasure.

Soon. Soon.

He followed the gleam of the chestnut hair that bounced in loose waves down her back. She led him on a merry chase without even knowing it, when she turned down the hall and into the kitchens. Ambrose ducked back out of sight before she could have seen him. The scrape of wood against stone told him she'd pulled back a chair from one of the counters. After the clink of silverware and a moan of pleasure, he simply couldn't continue denying himself the view of whatever she was doing. He purposely stumbled into the kitchen, as though surprised to find himself there.

Alex froze, fork poised near her parted lips, a chunk of what looked like blackberry tart speared on the fork tines. Her lashes flared up, her eyes unusually wide as she watched him.

"So sorry to interrupt...uh...what is it exactly you are

doing?" He glanced about the kitchens before approaching the opposite side of the counter and taking a seat facing her.

Alex was as red as a cherry. "Mrs. Cooper always leaves me a tart after the balls. She knows I get hungry because we don't have a chance to eat while all of the dancing goes on."

"Smart woman, your cook. Mind if I have a bite?" He plucked the fork out of her hand and dipped it into his mouth.

"Hmmm, that's good. Truly exquisite, like being in bed with a courtesan."

The look on her face was worth his rather colorful choice of words.

To his surprise, Alex laughed. "You are comparing food to...to that?"

"Food and sex? Absolutely, my dear. They are even better together, though."

The responding enlarged pupils of her eyes made his mouth water. Alex was a fascinating contradiction. A virgin, but a woman who felt desire quite strongly and was aware of how there could be pleasure in bed for both partners, not just the man. A woman who knew about sex but hadn't experienced it. A rare find in her level of society.

She was curious—he could see that in the way she watched him steal another bite of her tart and lick his lips. She wasn't in the least bit afraid of him. Skittish, perhaps, of physical contact, but not afraid. She was terrified of his reputation, but of him? No. And it was a rare woman who could separate the two.

"I think you say these things on purpose to unbalance me." Alex crossed her arms under her breasts, which only pressed her breasts up, giving him a much better view.

"You're right, Alex, love. I find the task of unbalancing you deliciously challenging." He would love to unbalance her right back onto the counter and feast on her rather than the tart, but it was still too soon.

"Have you ever had a decent conversation with a woman? One you weren't attempting to seduce?"

The question caught him off guard. Her bluntness was an admirable trait.

"Of course," he scoffed.

"Really? With whom?" she challenged.

He blustered for a moment. "With my mother and sister."

"You have a sister?" Alex uncrossed her arms and leaned forward, eyes bright with interest.

"Yes. Violet is seventeen. Just had her first season. I was beating men off with a stick. Though I suspect that has more to do with her inheritance. She's lovely, but shy." Ambrose loved Violet. She was a little darling.

There was something about little sisters, the way they were a brother's constant shadow. He'd never minded that she'd followed him about, and they'd shared more than one adventure when they visited friends in the country, until Violet had been deemed too old to chase after him in the fields. He had hated that she'd grown up, hated that she'd become a beautiful young woman who would someday marry a man and leave home. He wouldn't have ever admitted it aloud, but Violet was as dear a friend to him as Vaughn had once been. And when she married, her life would be full of children and she'd forget all about him. The thought filled his heart with a thick heaviness. She was polite, kind, and thoughtful. Any man who thought he deserved her would have to pass some highly rigorous tests of character before Ambrose would approve of the match. If he didn't think a man was up to snuff, he would advise their father against the man.

"Is she in Edinburgh with your parents?" Alex asked.

He shook his head and returned the fork to her. To his amusement, she didn't discard it but took another bite. There was something about them sharing a fork that made his blood heat. It was intimate, yet not in the way he was used to.

"She's still in London. Poor thing is living with our aunt Gertrude." Ambrose pitied his sister for that. If it wasn't an issue of supervision, he'd take Violet to his bachelor quarters on Jermyn Street, but that simply wasn't done.

Alex took another bite of the tart and sighed again with obvious pleasure. The lady had a sweet tooth; he rather liked the thought of that. Feeding a woman sweets was a pleasurable experience for them both, especially when he could taste the sugar upon her lips during a kiss...

"I take it your aunt Gertrude is difficult?"

He snorted. "Difficult is putting it politely. The woman has a room filled with just bonnets. Don't even ask me about her shoes. Violet has little interest in fashion, and spending time with Gertrude must be torture. I'm sure they shop on Bond Street every day!" He cringed at the thought. Violet would much rather find a bookshop and spend hours tucked away in a corner, reading about some ancient philosophy or science.

Alex chuckled but then sobered. "I know what that's like, to be trapped in the city with someone who does not share your taste in amusements. Perhaps someday I might meet your sister in London." Alex reached across the table, her hand catching his, unaware of her actions until it was too late. Ambrose could have pushed her in that moment, but he thought better of it. His skin burned where she touched him, and he didn't want her to remove her hand. So he simply covered her hand with his and responded honestly, without an attempt to seduce or charm her.

"I'm sure my sister would like that." He then rose from the table, disconnecting their hands.

The look of disappointment that flickered in her blue eyes didn't escape him. She had enjoyed their contact as much as he had. He circled around the table and came over to her, bracing one hand on the table beside her. Then he leaned in and brushed his lips over the crown of her head.

"What was that for?" she asked.

"For an enjoyable evening, Alex." He took his leave, hating to walk away from an opportunity. But Alex was a woman who needed a soft-handed seduction. Once she was his, though...he'd take her in a thousand places, in a thousand ways. He would stoke her inner fire until she was an unstoppable inferno of passion.

The little hellion would be a delight in bed. But tonight he was happy to leave his body unsatisfied, as the rest of him had thoroughly enjoyed their conversation. It was different when he talked to her. He never spoke of his family to ladies he wished to bed—that made a woman desire emotional intimacy. He didn't fear Alex would fall in love with him. He wouldn't let her. The wager required her seduction and ruination, but he wanted to enjoy being with her. He stopped dead just outside his room, shocked at what he'd just realized.

I enjoyed being with a woman outside of bed. That was a first. Aside from his mother and sister, he found women altogether boring unless they were naked beneath him, yet Alex had him spellbound. Knowing this unsettled him.

Why? What made her so different from all the others? Half of him wanted to turn around and get straight back on his horse and return to London, but the rest of him was determined to stay and figure out what made Lady Alexandra Rockford so fascinating.

✵ 5 ✵

Ambrose was lost in a dream of kissing Alex in a garden. The wisteria bloomed on overhanging trellises above them, and she lay beneath him on a blanket, her cheeks flush with arousal and her lips parted. Those dreamy blue eyes, like the petals of corn-flowers, drew him deeper and deeper into her. Their lips met languidly, each kiss wet, soft, and impossibly hot. How long had it been since he'd reveled in a single kiss without anything more?

Too long...since he'd been a lad stealing kisses from an upstairs maid when he was seventeen. Back then, kisses had been the height of his erotic knowledge and the best thing in the world.

"Would you ruin me, Ambrose? Break my heart?" the dream Alex murmured, her fingertips tracing his jaw as he gazed down at her. Around them the scents of the earth, a mix of bitter earth and sweet blooms, was almost as drugging as her touch.

"I have to, love—better me than another man." His reply was soft as he stroked her collarbone with his index finger and watched the swells of her breasts lift and fall with each exhalation. "I have to..." he repeated, but the slowly growing guilt ate away at him.

Her lashes lowered and she closed her eyes. He dipped his head, ready to catch her lips with his—

A rap of knuckles on the door made Ambrose jolt awake in bed. The dim predawn light was a faint gray that barely penetrated the windows.

Lord, what time was it?

"Yes?" he called out when the knocking came again.

The door opened, and Ben, the footman who attended him last night, carried in a tray.

"I'm so sorry, my lord. I am here with your breakfast, per your request." Ben approached the bed and set the tray across Ambrose's lap before he set about pulling away the thick damask curtains on the bed, letting only a feeble bit of light in.

"My request?" Ambrose stared at the large bowl with blue flower-patterned china sitting on the tray next to a glass of juice.

"Er...yes," Ben replied, a little shy. "Your morning porridge to be served at six in the morning. Our cook, Mrs. Cooper, prepared it especially for you, to your liking."

Ambrose's gaze dropped to the offending bowl, and with a sigh, he picked up the spoon and dipped it in. Maybe some porridge wouldn't be too bad. He'd be able to go down and eat with the rest of the house in a few hours. He blew on the steamy porridge and then slipped the spoon in his mouth.

A bitter, salty taste hit his taste buds like a blow to the face.

"Ack!" He spewed out the vile-tasting concoction and snatched the cloth napkin off his tray and wiped at his mouth.

Ben had been in the midst of laying out a new set of trousers and froze, his eyes wide as he stared at Ambrose.

"Who said I requested this?" He waved at the bowl, still smacking his lips before he took a very, very long gulp of juice. It barely erased the over-salted porridge.

"Um..." Ben shuffled his feet. "I was told by the house-keeper, who was told by the cook, who I believe was informed by Lady Alexandra."

"You've got to be..." His words trailed off into a low growl.

"Right...well, I'll just leave you to eat..." Ben started to back out the door, his face a little pale.

Ambrose let him go. He could tell the lad was fright-ened, and Ambrose knew why. He was letting his anger bubble up to the surface, but the only one who would pay for this was Alex, and he was going to be ruthless...by making her desperate for him. He wouldn't go easy or slow

—he'd take over her senses and overwhelm her with passion.

Alex, love, you've set the rules for our game, and I intend to win.

❧

Alex was perched on the edge of her seat, delicately licking off the last bit of honey from her fingertips, when the dining room door opened. Ambrose strode in, his tall, lean legs finely on display in buckskin trousers. He tugged absentmindedly at his gold-and-cream striped waistcoat as he scanned the room. When his eyes settled upon her, he smiled.

"Ah, breakfast," he announced and came over to sit directly across from her. "I'm simply famished." He reached for the tray of toast and then added bacon and eggs to his plate.

Carefully wiping her hands on her napkin, Alex sipped her tea and studied him. His hair was a little mussed, as though he'd run his hands through it. The dark strands revealed a hint of red when the midmorning sunlight illuminated them. How curious. Her hands itched to reach out and touch his hair, to get a closer look. She abruptly shook herself out of such strange daydreams.

"How did you sleep, Mr. Worthing?" she inquired, knowing all too well that poor Ben had woken him up four hours earlier with salty porridge. The footman had rushed straight to the cook, who'd told the housekeeper, who'd come to Alex, distraught over having upset their guest. Alex had assured the woman that their guest was not at all upset, even though she knew he was. But that had been the point of it all. To infuriate him into leaving.

"I slept well enough, thank you for asking." He hummed softly as he spread marmalade on his toast, and Alex's lips parted in shock. That hadn't been the response she'd been expecting. So he wasn't going to admit he'd been woken up far too early? Interesting...

"And you?" he asked. "Did you sleep well? I imagine dining on tarts before bed might give you sweet dreams." His brown eyes were as warm as the honey in the pot beside her.

Startled by his lack of reaction to her scheming, she answered honestly. "No...the rain...the sound of it on the rooftops and the gables makes me restless." She shivered at the memory, and his eyes darkened.

"Are you sure you slept well? I see dark circles under your eyes." She tested him, seeing if he would mention the little morning surprise she'd planned.

"Well enough." His look sharpened as though he sensed what she was fishing for.

"You could skip the shoot my father had planned." She smiled smugly as she thought of Ambrose missing out on an activity he clearly favored.

"No, I'll be quite fine. I'm resilient, you see," he

murmured, his voice a little too low to be prudent over breakfast.

She blinked, trying to think of a response, but she had none.

"And I shall also be attending Lady Darby's picnic in a week, so if you're in a mind to pester me into leaving, you'll be sorely disappointed, my love." He chuckled when she huffed in outrage.

"I would never pester you into leaving, Mr. Worthing. You're my father's guest, and it's not the sort of thing a lady with good breeding would do." She raised her chin and met his amused gaze defiantly.

"I believe it is the exact sort of thing you'd do, Alex."

She glowered at him, and before he could say anything else, she fled the room.

THE NEXT WEEK PASSED IN A BLUR. ALEX KEPT HERSELF in check when it came to punishing her guest outright. She didn't want him to know that she had been attempting to push him into leaving. That meant she'd played the dutiful daughter and a gracious hostess to the rakehell. And for the last seven days, she had to admit, the man had been charming and likeable.

When they weren't quarreling about everything, she realized they agreed on quite a few things. He too loved the outdoors, and more than once she'd found him catching up to her when she took her horse out in the mornings for a ride. Sometimes they talked, and sometimes they didn't. The silence then was amiable too, and it reminded her of what he'd said about his friend Gareth and how friendships could form like this between two people.

Was it possible for the daughter of an earl and a notorious rakehell to be friends? If she ignored his teasing hints that he would dearly love to seduce her, she could almost imagine that they were in fact becoming friends.

Now, as she sat at the breakfast table contemplating how much she did in fact enjoy spending time with Ambrose, she realized her foolishness.

It was like falling in love with Marshall all over again. If she wasn't careful she might put her heart in danger, and that was the *very last thing* she wished to do. Ambrose had made her lower her guard, as any good rogue would do with an unsuspecting lady.

She needed to fight back, regain control of the situation before she found herself embroiled in a scandal she couldn't recover from. It was bad enough to be a friend of a rake, but it was even worse to be romantically tied to one, even by rumors and gossip.

Whilst she was busy woolgathering, Ambrose had slipped into the dining room, his hand containing a single flower. He took the seat beside her and leaned over, delicately tucking the flower behind her ear. His fingertips burned her skin deliciously where he touched her ear, and then he caressed her cheek with the back of his knuckles.

"I missed you on the morning ride. Why didn't you wait for me?" he asked.

Her heart gave a little treacherous leap as she carefully removed the flower from behind her ear and examined it.

A snowdrop. Her favorite.

"Why did you bring me this?" Her voice was soft, breathless.

His gaze moved from the flower to her lips and then settled upon her eyes. "Because you said they were your favorite. *Galanthus nivalis.* The snowdrop. Pale and beautiful, alluring and sweet with a hint of winter, like you."

"A hint of winter?" She was staring at him, trying to decide if that was an insult or a compliment.

"Hmmm," he hummed. "Winter is a beautiful season. Everything is silver and light and filled with mystery. When I think of you, I think of those quiet mornings when snow has freshly covered the forest trails and everything feels different, new, and mysterious."

She knew just what he meant about the winter. It was why she loved winter above other seasons. So many ladies her age loved the springtime or the fall, but for her, winter and its mysterious moods had always captivated her—just like Ambrose was captivating her.

"I..." She cleared her throat, still clutching the snowdrop and feeling foolish for not wanting to let it go.

"Lady Darby's picnic is this afternoon. I assume you're

attending?" He didn't move away from her, but remained scandalously close.

"The picnic? Of course," she replied hastily. If she didn't regain control of herself soon, she would make a mistake. It was time to return to her pranks and send this rakehell back to London before she did something stupid like fall in love. She had one more trick to play on Ambrose, and that thought restored her spirits.

"I'm afraid I must go early to assist Perdita with a personal matter. You'll need to be careful in finding your way to the picnic spot. It's not at Darby House, you see, but on some land a mile north. There's a lovely hill, and you can see much of the village below. I would be happy to draw up some directions for you." Her voice was falsely cheerful as she inwardly hated the thought that she was renewing her plans to drive him away, but it was for the best.

His eyes narrowed but his lips curved. "Thank you, I'd like that."

He doesn't trust me. She could see it in his eyes, but he was attempting to fool her. Clever man.

"I'm surprised you aren't trying to convince me not to come to the picnic," he mused.

She shrugged. "It's not as though you'd do as I wished, and your being here has enlivened my father in a way I've not seen in quite some time. I'd be a terrible daughter if I drove you away when he was so happy." That was true— she was a terrible daughter for wishing Ambrose gone when he did make her father so clearly delighted. But Ambrose was tempting her, and she didn't *want* to be tempted. Not after Marshall had broken her heart. She was done being a fool in love.

"I am glad to be visiting. Your father was a good man to me when I was a lad," Ambrose admitted. More honesty. That continued to surprise Alex. "It's strange to think that I came here as a child while you were tucked away in a crib in the nursery." He chuckled softly, and the sound was rich and inviting.

It was indeed strange to think of it. Alex hadn't been able to get it out of her head that one of London's most infamous rakes had been scrambling about Rockford House as a lad, likely carrying frogs in his pockets and chasing geese down the garden path that led to the small pond where her father loved to fish in the summer. The image made her smile.

"You're smiling," Ambrose observed as he took a sip of his coffee.

She was, and she wouldn't deny it. "I was picturing you as a boy, wondering what sort of trouble you likely got into while you were here."

Ambrose lifted his chin loftily. "Nonsense. I was the most perfectly-behaved boy in all of England."

There was no helping it—she giggled. "Liar." She covered her mouth to stifle more giggles. She'd never met a man who made her laugh so much. It was delightful.

"Fair enough, I was a terrible little boy, full of tricks,

but I had a good heart, I assure you of that. I never struck a bird with a slingshot or threw stones at stray cats," he replied in all seriousness.

"That I do believe." She couldn't picture him as a wild and cruel child, no matter that he was a breaker of hearts now.

"And what of you, Alex? What were you like as a child?" He leaned back in his chair and steepled his fingers as he studied her. "Buried up to your nose in books? Or were you dashing about the hills, dirtying your dress?" He said this in such a warm, genuine tone she found she wanted to reply honestly.

"I've always loved to read, but I was very much a girl who did dash about the hills, dirtying more than one dress." She smiled fondly, thinking that she was still that sort of woman who ran through the fields. "Perdita and I used to read a lot together as children when we weren't getting into trouble in the fields. Her father and mine built us a house among the branches of a tree at the edge of the garden. It was a quaint little place where we tucked ourselves away and read for hours." Those sunny memories of the little house in the trees had been some of her favorite days.

"You and Perdita are close?" he asked, leaning forward slightly.

She nodded. "We are as close as sisters, but without the competition that some sisters have. Neither of us has any desire to marry, and we've never been jealous over gentlemen. We just..." She struggled for the right word. "We make sense together. I'm afraid I can't explain it."

Ambrose nodded. "I know what you mean. You can sit together in a room for hours in silence and simply enjoy each other's company. My friend Gareth is like that for me. I could sit late into the night in his evening room with him, drinking brandy and not having to speak a word. But that's changed..." His face darkened with emotion.

"In what way?" she prompted, wondering if he'd answer or if he'd lock his secrets back up in his heart.

"He's married now. Wonderful woman, Helen, but it's not the same when I'm with him. There's a part of him that misses her even for a moment when she's out of the room. I can see it in his eyes. It's not that he's unnaturally attached, per se...I'm bungling this." He chuckled wryly. "But it's more that they so complete each other that they miss the other when they are separated."

That was something she had understood once, long ago...with Marshall. That need to be with him, even when he was across the room. After he'd left for London, she'd felt as though she'd wasted away without him. But in time, she'd realized she'd been too young, too foolish. A girl of seventeen didn't always know the difference between infatuation and love. And while one was more lasting and deeper than the other, the pain of the break was same. She had vowed never to let another man hurt her like that again.

Even now she sensed her foolish heart wanting to give

Ambrose a chance, let him inside so he might shatter her when he left. It was too dangerous, this sharing of memories and talk of childhoods.

She rose from her chair, and he stood as well. "Please, sit, finish your breakfast." She gestured to his chair, and he did so reluctantly. Even rakes could still be gentlemen every now and then.

"I'd be happy to go with you to the Darbys' early," he offered.

Shaking her head, she backed away. "No, I insist, please stay. I'll write some directions for you to the picnic spot and leave them with a footman."

"Very well." He was still watching her, and she knew that the intimacy between them was thinning again, as though both she and Ambrose were fortifying the walls around their hearts.

She inwardly shook herself at the thought as she slipped from the dining room into the corridor. *Who knew I would have so much in common with a rake?*

🙎 6 🙎

Bloody hell.

Ambrose was standing in a cow-covered field.

The sloping hill he stood upon was filled with cows, a breed he recognized from his father's talk of livestock whenever he came back from school for weekends in the country. White Park cows had curved horns and rich white hides speckled with faint black dots. They were fairly docile beasts, but being in the midst of them was unsettling.

Lifting the scrap of parchment again, Ambrose stared at the directions the footman had provided him. He hadn't been foolish enough to trust Alex's word, so he'd asked the footman to confirm the directions.

South down the lane, past the wooden gatehouse, turn right onto the garden path, and straight into the forest for a quarter of a mile...then climb the hill...

He muttered the last few words aloud and wiped at his brow. The hike had brought on a sweat. Not that he was unused to physical exertions—he boxed and fenced regularly—but he wasn't dressed for walking about the hills and valleys of Lothbrook.

"Where the bloody hell is the picnic?"

"Sir? Are you lost?" A little voice drew Ambrose's attention, and he found a lad standing at the edge of the field about fifteen feet away. He carried a makeshift fishing pole and a cloth bag full of fish.

"Lad, do you know the way to Darby House?" he asked, walking toward the lad.

Squelch!

Ambrose slid and nearly fell onto his backside. He recovered his balance and stared down to see his new boots covered in cow manure.

The boy chortled and then gasped, covering his mouth. Ambrose almost started laughing too.

"Darby House is..." The boy was holding his stomach now with one hand to keep from laughing. "About a mile in the other direction, sir."

He should have known. "Of course it is." Ambrose wiped one boot on the grass, trying to remove the essence of the cows, but it was no use. He was going to show up at the Darbys' picnic smelling like cow dung.

Had the footman given him the wrong directions? Ambrose searched his mind, playing back that moment when the young man had stared at the directions Ambrose asked him to verify and he'd quickly nodded.

"That looks true to me, sir!" the footman had said before he'd rushed off to his duties.

Surely Lady Alexandra Rockford did not stoop to involving her own staff in plots to make him angry. Lady Alexandra might not...but his cunning little Alex certainly would. And after all that talk this morning, when he'd felt he was coming to know her. He crumpled the directions in his palm. When he got hold of her at the picnic, he was going to get his revenge for this.

The entire walk back, Ambrose plotted his revenge for Alex's trick. How he would get her alone away from the rest of the country folk and show her just what it meant to be the full focus of his attention. By the time he found Darby House, the rest of the town and the surrounding gentry had assembled on the lawn in front of the large Georgian country house. Tents had been erected, and tables with tea were already crowded with ladies and gentlemen. The light breeze tugged at the ladies' skirts, making the fabric shape to their bodies. It was quite a sight when he noticed Alex by the tea tables, talking avidly with Perdita. Both ladies were distractedly pulling at their skirts while laughing.

She was lovely—there was no denying that now. He'd thought her passingly pretty before, but the more time he spent around her, the more times she frustrated him and challenged him, the more he found he admired her...

admired and *desired* her. He wanted to cup that little chin of hers and brush his thumbs over her cheeks and watch her eyes darken as he bent his head to kiss her.

When she glanced his way, he flashed her a wolfish grin before he headed toward where a group of men stood by one of the large fountains.

"Ambrose, my boy, over here!" Rockford waved him over, a broad smile and merriment dancing in his eyes.

It was impossible to ignore the sudden blossom of warmth in his chest at being welcomed so openly by the older man. Rockford was very much like his own father, a kind man who never went without friends. A little voice in the back of Ambrose's mind raised a question.

Why aren't you the same? What made you so cold and distant?

He and his friend Gareth had once been happy young men at Eton together and later at university, but somewhere between leaving school and growing up they'd lost their inner joy. Gareth had of course married and lost his wife in childbirth. That would break even the strongest of men. But now he had Helen and was the old Gareth that Ambrose believed he'd never see again.

I haven't lost anyone. I was never in love or married. So what makes me so cold?

He stilled just as he reached the group of men by the fountain. He had lost someone. He and Gareth had been close friends with Vaughn, who was now Viscount Darlington.

Vaughn's father had passed away, leaving Vaughn with a

mountain of debt, and he'd sought to recover himself in whatever way he could, often through winning small fortunes from other men during games of chance—not that it worked well in the long term. The Darlington estate was still impoverished. And when Vaughn had slipped into this less honorable means of obtaining coin, it had pushed both Gareth and Ambrose away from him. They hadn't been able to stomach his harsh methods of keeping his family estate intact. It was hard to stand by a man who would financially break other men with gambling debts. But it was never enough to keep Darlington House safe from creditors. Vaughn needed a rich wife who would provide him with plenty of funds.

More than once Ambrose and Gareth had sought to convince Vaughn to part with his family's home and sell it. But he'd refused to even entertain the idea and had severed ties with them.

Losing his friend had been dreadful, and his heart had turned to ice.

"Glad to see you found your way! Didn't get lost, did you?" Rockford teased as he clapped a hand on Ambrose's shoulder when he fully entered the circle of men.

"Lost? No, definitely not." He chuckled and cast one knowing glance toward Alex, who was still watching him.

Soon he'd catch her alone and they would have a discussion about her devilish tactics to upset him. A discussion that would involve a fair amount of kisses.

Normally Alex would have enjoyed Lady Darby's picnic, but not today. She was sleep-deprived and grumpy.

"You look dreadful," Perdita murmured when Alex joined her by the tea tables.

"Do I? I certainly feel it." She knew she must look poorly if her friend was telling her so. Her reflection this morning had been that of a pale woman with dark circles under her eyes. It had been impossible to sleep with Ambrose down the hall. And this morning they'd talked again as they had the night before in the kitchens, sharing parts of themselves with each other. The intimacy of those moments had frightened her. The man had shown her a great affection for his mother and sister and a childhood full of happy memories that matched her own.

We each guard our own hearts. That common ground unsettled her.

"But I do have something that will cheer us up. I've set in motion plans to drive Mr. Worthing back to London!"

Her friend covered her mouth. "Oh no, Alex, what have you done?"

"Just a few things…I gave him false directions to send him to Mr. Merryweather's cow field rather than to your house. If my plans succeed, he might miss the picnic altogether."

Perdita and Alex both started laughing.

"That's terribly wicked of you. But I don't understand.

I thought perhaps you and Mr. Worthing might have decided you rather liked each other and were not mortal enemies." Perdita looked down, running a palm over her pale-green walking dress.

"Like each other? Good heavens, Perdita, I certainly don't like him."

Perdita poured herself a new cup of tea and dropped two lumps of sugar into it. "I was quite convinced you might...because well..."

"Because..." Alex focused on her friend, wondering what Perdita meant. The fact that her dearest friend seemed to think she and Ambrose liked each other was not reassuring.

"You didn't sleep with Mr. Worthing, did you?" Perdita changed the subject slightly, and Alex didn't like where this question was headed.

Alex blanched. "No! Of course I didn't. Why would you say that?"

Her friend's cheeks pinkened. "Oh, Alex, I'm sorry. I didn't mean anything by it, I just thought after the dance a week ago...you and he seemed so...Well, it seems he escaped Mr. Merryweather's cows..." Perdita didn't finish. Her eyes were focused on something behind Alex.

Alex turned her head in the direction of her friend's attention. There was a group of men near a fountain at the center of the garden. Ambrose had just arrived, and when he saw her, he smiled at her. The expression was predatory, but rather than scaring her, it made her skin flush and her body tingle in secret places.

After a moment of them simply staring at each other, he made his way to the group of men, which included her father. He was clapped on the back and welcomed amongst the men. He immediately settled into their set and raised one booted foot on the edge of the fountain, and he was leaning in, one forearm braced on his raised knee. He started speaking, and from what Alex could see the men of Lothbrook were listening avidly, her father included.

Alex sighed and turned back to Perdita. "We did see each other after the ball."

Perdita's gaze whipped back to her. "But you said…"

"We only talked. He found me in the kitchen, eating my post-ball tart."

"You talked?" Perdita chuckled. "What do rakes talk about?"

"Apparently their sisters." Alex couldn't suppress a grin at the memory.

"Mr. Worthing has a sister?" Perdita perked up this news, and it made Alex admit how much she would miss Perdita. She would be leaving for London in a few weeks because her mother was determined to take her to some dinner parties and balls in hopes of snaring a desperate impoverished aristocrat. Perdita's father was only a country gentleman, and her mother was in a constant quest for a higher title.

"Yes, Violet sounds like quite a dear. Apparently she's living with an aunt who's obsessed with fashion."

"It's a pity you could not invite her here. That would certainly be one way to kill his ardor. Surely he wouldn't seduce you while his sister is here."

"Seduce me? Perdita, he's not going to do that."

Perdita's brows rose, but neither of them spoke as two ladies came over to the tea tables to retrieve some sandwiches. Alex and her friend sipped their tea, nodded at the other ladies, and murmured polite hellos. Once the ladies had moved along, Perdita leaned in close to Alex.

"Mr. Worthing's reaction to you at the dance says otherwise. He looked like he wanted to eat you like *you* were the delicious tart."

"Perdy!" Alex burst out laughing.

The men near the fountain turned their way, curious to see what had caused her to burst out in such loud amusement. Ambrose's brown eyes were warm and dark as they settled on her. Something equally warm and dark stirred in Alex. His gaze promised heady kisses, roving hands, and passionate domination.

"You're blushing, dear," Perdita whispered around her cup of tea.

Alex blinked and ducked her head. The men around Ambrose broke apart, and he headed their way.

"Should we ask him about Mr. Merryweather's cows?" Perdita whispered through giggles.

"Oh hush!" Alex bit her lip to keep from snickering.

That would be most unladylike, even though she felt quite compelled to jump with glee.

"Ladies." Ambrose inclined his head.

"Mr. Worthing." Perdita rose and glanced at Alex. "Anyone need more tea?" she offered.

Alex and Ambrose both shook their heads.

The second Perdita had walked away to the farthest tea table, leaving them alone, Ambrose held out a hand to Alex.

"Walk with me?"

It was a terrible idea, she knew it, but she couldn't help it. She placed her hand in his, allowing him to draw her up. He tucked her arm in his, the action drawing them close, the intimacy of it heating her inside.

"I'm simply dying to know what you and Miss Darby were laughing about." Ambrose led her through the meandering rows of rose bushes and toward a distant archway that led away from the gardens.

"We weren't talking about you, if that's what you believe." Alex's tone was slightly defensive, but that was because she felt quite guilty that they had been doing just that.

"Actually, I do believe that."

They reached the archway and walked through it. Behind them the garden remained full of the guests, but ahead of her and Ambrose, there was a wooded glen.

"Where are we going?" Alex drew up short as she realized they were almost out of sight and shouting distance of the remainder of the guests.

"We're going to have it out, my dear. It's time we had a little chat about salty porridge, cow fields, and it's about damned time I did this…"

He spun her around, and she was swept toward his mouth as he claimed her with a kiss.

7

Ambrose captured Alex's lips in a ravenous kiss. She thumped her hands against his chest in a mixture of shock and protestation, but when he cupped her face in his hands and deepened the kiss, his rough fingers against her skin, she had to admit she didn't want him to stop.

A thrill shot through her as she felt his tongue trace the seam of her lips, probing against the line of her mouth, and she wondered what she was meant to do. She was so new to this type of intimacy, and he was so practiced. She closed her eyes in wonder, waiting to experience what he would teach her with his hands and mouth next.

"Open for me, love," he murmured against her mouth, and she did.

A little gasp escaped her when his tongue slipped inside her lips. Her tongue sought his, playing with it, and she reveled in the wicked sensation of how it felt to kiss a man like this. It wasn't chaste, wasn't sweet. It was a raw, carnal, pleasurable kiss she didn't want to end.

Ambrose curled one arm around her waist, panting softly as he moved her backward. She tripped over a clump of grass, and they tumbled to the ground. They shared a startled laugh, but Ambrose demanded her attention again, molding her body to his beneath him. He slowed his gentle assault on her senses, drawing back to gaze down at her. Propped on his elbows as he was, hips pressing against hers, she was fully trapped, yet the questioning in his eyes undid her. She knew in that moment if she demanded he let her up, he would have let her go. It was reassuring, and yet she felt in charge too, which made her feel safe, even when they were doing something that could lead to her ruination if they were discovered.

"God, you're beautiful," he whispered.

He bent his head, licked her lips, and nibbled them. Alex whimpered, rolling her hips against his, seeking something she barely understood. It was hard to describe, but from the moment he kissed her, she'd begun to surrender to the wild urges rising from the darkness inside her, a wicked need to feel him, to lie skin to skin with him in the grass and not care what anyone would think.

"You're killing me, sweetheart," he growled in warning.

"It hurts...it's throbbing," she confessed against his neck. She nipped his right earlobe before she pressed kisses to his neck. His skin was slightly salty from a faint sheen of sweat, and she found that strangely erotic. He wasn't some fantasy she'd dreamed up—he was a real man who was kissing her, driving her mad with desire.

His hands turned frantic, tugging at her gown, rucking it up past her hips. Ambrose shoved her petticoats up until he got one hand into her drawers and cupped her mound. She jolted at the sudden possessive but gentle touch.

"Tell me no if you want me to stop," he murmured between kisses against her lips.

"No, don't...stop..." She panted hard as she sought to adjust to the wild building of excitement in her body. This was absolutely a terrible idea, and she couldn't fathom why she wanted him to touch her and kiss her when they'd only known each other for a day, but there was something about him that drove her a little mad...

Ambrose stole another kiss before he slipped one finger between her thighs and into her.

"Oh!" She jerked at the feeling of the intrusion. It was frightening and exciting and strange. He was touching her there, inside. She shivered and clung to him, watching his eyes, searching for any hint that he would take it too far before she was ready. But only a gentle, burning hunger was in his gaze, and it was layered with an urgency she felt inside herself.

"Shh...relax for me, sweetheart," he encouraged.

She cupped his face and kissed him, relaxing into his touch.

Alex's breath left her in a soft rush when he began to slide his finger in and out. His penetration of her deepened and quickened. Ambrose commanded a mastery of her, with hands and lips, creating a physical symphony of pleasure. It built and built, the tension inside her wound tight as a band. When his tongue began to mimic the thrusting erotic play of his finger, it was too much for her body to bear. Alex shattered into a million glittering stars, her release tearing through her like a strong tide.

When she finally drifted down to earth, she was dimly aware of Ambrose's hand leaving her and pulling her skirts down to her knees. He was groaning as he shifted on the ground.

"Bloody hell, I won't be able to walk for a minute," he panted in obvious frustration.

Confused, Alex looked over at his lap and then saw the bulge in his trousers. "Are you...do you need me to..." She had to admit she was rather fascinated by the idea of touching him in the way he had intimately touched her. He'd pleasured her, and surely it was only fair that she reciprocate—not that she had any idea what to do except touch him.

Ambrose threw his head back and sighed. "I won't ask that of you, love. You're sweet to offer, but..." He shook his head.

"I want to." She reached for the placket of his trousers before he could stop her, and his body responded by jerking at her exploring touch.

"Fuck!" His rough curse would have made her blush if her own face wasn't already flaming from her determination to discover the secrets of his body.

"What do I do?" she asked in a husky whisper, her fingers trailing down the length of his erect shaft.

A fierce light lit his eyes as he watched her tease him lightly with her touch.

"You've got to stroke me, sweetheart, please." He leaned forward, burying his face in the heaving valley of her breasts as he placed one hand on hers, guiding her through the motions. He rocked against her body, echoing the movement of lovemaking as her hand kept a firm grip around the silken hard length of his shaft.

Ambrose raised his head as he reached the moment of his glorious completion, his eyes locking with hers. What she saw there robbed her of her breath. Raw, exquisite desire, mixed with shock and something soft in his gaze. He was beautiful, a god, and he was rocking between her parted thighs as though she were his personal heaven. Something hot splashed on her hand, and Ambrose growled in pleasure, shuddered, and then collapsed heavily on top of her.

Panting, he rested his head on her breasts again, nuzzling the flushed peaks barely concealed by her gown. Surely there was nothing better in the world than this, the warm sun on her bare skin, the feel of cool grass like silk beneath her and Ambrose's weight on top of her. He pressed soft kisses to her cheek, his breath shallow and slow as though he was ready to fall asleep. Every muscle in her body was relaxed, and she felt languid, almost lazy. It would have taken Mrs. Darby and a parade of the rest of Lothbrook's matrons to make her even lift her head.

The sudden image of those matrons made Alex twitch, and clarity started to pierce the delightful haze in her head. Mrs. Darby or anyone else could stroll this way and spot them!

Rationality began to inch back in bit by agonizing bit. She was lying just outside the garden with a coldhearted rake between her legs, and her life could be destroyed if anyone saw them.

"What have we done?" she gasped, struggling to push him off. With a groan of protest, he moved off her and lay flat on his back, uncaring that his male parts were completely exposed.

"We've just had one of the best picnics ever." He chuckled, a schoolboy grin making him utterly irresistible when he glanced her away.

Alex had to stop herself from smiling back. Pulling herself together, she slapped his shoulder. "For heaven's sake, fix your trousers! You're flapping about in the wind, and someone could see us! See you!" She couldn't imagine what horrors would follow if the Lothbrook matrons caught sight of Ambrose's sizable male appendage while he stretched out in the grass like some Italian lothario. It might strike them dead with fear or shock them with the scandal.

With a sensual chuckle, he fixed his trousers and then palmed one of her bare thighs possessively. "Enjoy the afterglow, sweetheart. You can tear me to pieces later."

Alex wanted to argue, but when he reached up, clapped a hand over her mouth, and dragged her to lie back down in the grass beside him, she stilled and relaxed. He released her mouth and stroked a little pattern on her collarbones.

It felt good—too good.

"Just relax for a minute," he encouraged. "Don't let what we've done go to waste. This is sometimes just as good as the moment of ecstasy itself." He seemed almost surprised when he admitted this.

"Do you not often lie like this afterward?" she asked him, laying one hand on his chest. The silk of his waist-coat was soft beneath her fingers, and she marveled at the intricate stitching of the beautiful garment.

"I...not usually," he said with a sigh. "I rarely feel this... sated." A little smile curved his lips, and for some reasons Alex loved that smile more because it wasn't forced, nor was it false. He was being himself with her, just Ambrose, not a rake intent on leaving a trail of broken hearts behind him.

She and Ambrose lay together, bodies pressed close, their breaths mingling, neither of them speaking. Every few minutes her body would twitch, her inner muscles spasming with an aftershock of pleasure.

"I take it that was your first time to climax?" Ambrose

asked after a moment. She gave a shaky nod. "And what did you think?"

Alex laughed softly. "I can see why people are always guarding us unmarried ladies from men like you. You're dangerous. *This*"—she waved between their bodies—"is dangerous."

Ambrose tightened his arm on her waist and sighed. "I'm going to take that as a compliment."

She thought they would get up soon, but Ambrose kept hold of her, and she liked feeling so close to him. He brushed a stray curl away from her cheek.

"Alex, why haven't you been to London? You didn't debut. The daughter of an earl would be in high demand during the season." The backs of his knuckles stroked her cheek, and then he cupped her chin. His other hand toyed with the fabric of her gown, the actions far too intimate, the sort of thing a lover would do.

"I don't care for London. I like the country."

"Alex," he warned softly. "I know it's more than that. You've never made an attempt on the marriage mart. Why?"

Alex flushed. She didn't want to talk about Marshall or how her heart had never recovered from the pain of his breaking off their secret engagement. Going to London would mean facing Marshall and her past heartache.

"I should go. We've been gone too long already. Someone might notice."

Ambrose sat up, eyeing her skeptically. "You're allowed

to have your secrets, sweetheart. Lord knows I've enough secrets to fill an entire townhouse on Half Moon Street. But people are talking."

"People are talking?" Lord, she sounded shrill. "What people?"

"People." He glanced away.

"Who?" She grabbed his neckcloth and yanked, catching his attention.

"The men in the clubs."

"You mean I'm being talked about in the clubs?" That was completely taboo. Gentlemen weren't supposed to even utter a lady's name inside a gentlemen's club. And if they were talking, it was a bad thing. A very bad thing. A tremor of dread rippled through her, leaving an empty feeling inside her that seemed to grow larger each passing second.

"Yes, more or less."

She swallowed down the dread and tried to approach the matter as logically as she could and frowned at him. "Am I in the betting books?"

Ambrose's brows arched. "You know about those?"

"Of course I do. I'm not a half-wit. What are they betting on?"

He opened his mouth, his brown eyes suddenly guarded. Before he could answer, Perdita's voice on the other side of the garden wall was calling for them.

"We'd better go." He pulled her to her feet and checked her hair and gown for leaves and grass. When they were both presentable, Ambrose escorted her back to the garden.

Perdita rushed toward them, and her eyes widened. "Where have you two been? You'll never believe what's happened!" She was rambling so fast that Alex caught her friend's chin and gently squeezed until Perdita's face slackened, and she gazed at her friend with pursed lips.

"Sorry, Perdy, but you were rambling." Alex smiled and dropped her hand. "Now, what is it?"

"It's a scandal, that's what!"

Alex glanced in panic at Ambrose. Had they been seen? He gave her the slightest shrug.

"What scandal?"

"Viscount Darlington has arrived. No one invited him. He simply rode up in his coach and walked in! Mama fainted dead away when he bowed and kissed her hand. Every single lady is now circled around him. There's nothing like an impoverished titled gentleman with a body like a Roman god. You know every woman with a fortune would be happy to marry him. Lord, I hope my mother gets no ideas about buying a title for me. I should loathe being married to a man who wants me only for my money, no matter how beautiful he is to look at."

When Perdita finally stopped talking, Alex had a chance to breathe a sigh of relief. But when she looked to Ambrose, he wasn't calm. His shoulders were bunched, and his fists were slightly clenched.

As Perdita led them back to the Darby residence, Alex sidled closer to Ambrose.

"What's the matter?"

Ambrose's nostrils flared. "Darlington? Promise you will avoid him, Alex. He makes me look like bloody Prince Charming."

"I've heard he's dangerous, but I thought it was only to ladies."

"It's more than that. He's killed men in duels, and he's a dominating man, Alex. Do you understand me?"

Alex blinked. "I'm sure you mean he's just not very particular in his tastes…"

Ambrose groaned in exasperation. "He's the sort to tie a lady down and strike her on her arse, Alex. I don't want you anywhere near him. Promise me." He caught her arm, pulling her up short just before they entered the Darby gardens.

"As much as I would love to disagree with you, I think that perhaps you are right. I will stay clear of him."

Ambrose heaved a relieved sigh.

The sight that greeted them in the middle of the gardens was partly comical and partly shocking. A tall man with sun-kissed skin and ice-blond hair stood in the center of the gardens, arms crossed and glaring at the ring of ladies vying for his attentions. The cold gleam in his blue eyes froze Alex's blood. This was not a man to get cross-wise with. His muscled frame and large hands looked positively lethal, just as lethal as the seductive smile he flashed as he caught sight of her and Ambrose.

"Worthing. Good to see you again." Darlington inclined his head. The group of ladies all swirled about, momentarily distracted.

"Darlington."

Alex couldn't ignore the steel beneath Ambrose's velvet-soft voice.

Darlington waved an imperious hand, and the ladies chittering about him like colorful little birds parted so he could walk to Alex. He bent over her hand, his lips teasing her knuckles, his blond hair an enticing halo of color. When he raised his head, his blue eyes were rich sapphire pools, blazing with an inner fire.

"I've heard much about you, Lady Alexandra Rockford." Darlington released her hand and straightened.

"You have, have you?" Her tone was a little colder than was proper.

Alex had a sneaking suspicion he'd read the betting books as well. She may have been innocent in many ways, but she wasn't an idiot. Viscount Darlington's unexpected arrival in the quaint village of Lothbrook wasn't a coincidence. Whatever Ambrose had mentioned in the books had to do with her. Darlington likely had intentions to make a play for whatever the wager involved. She only feared what that wager would be if it worried a rakehell like Ambrose Worthing.

8

"What brings you to Lothbrook, Lord Darlington?" Alex asked, keeping her tone deliberately cool. She could feel the heat of Ambrose's body directly behind her, reminding her of what Ambrose had said about him being dangerous. If Darlington had showed up here of all places, it had to be for a specific reason—such as to win a wager in a betting book.

She was suddenly very glad that Ambrose was here. He may be a rake, but so far he had been an entirely honest one. This Lord Darlington, she sensed, would be quite the opposite. He had eyes made to hold secrets and lips that seemed made to speak sweet lies that would woo an innocent maid into a bad position. Ambrose was no less dangerous, but he never seemed to hide his desires or his intentions, and she respected him and trusted him on that alone.

"Oh, the need to bask in the idyllic countryside. London has grown tiresome, wouldn't you agree, Worthing?" As he spoke, his penetrating eyes darted away from her face to settle upon something just over her shoulder. His entire demeanor cast off a seemingly bored exterior, as he if couldn't bother to be here or rather anywhere at the moment, and Lothbrook would be as fine as any place.

Alex resisted the urge to follow his gaze. She knew instinctively that Darlington was looking at Ambrose.

"I disagree—London hosts many entertainments. Perhaps you are missing out on them and ought to return?" Ambrose suggested, his tone carrying a slight edge that went unmissed by Darlington.

The tension between the two men became noticeable enough to draw the focus of Perdita's mother and a group of other ladies standing not too far away. The distant twitter of the matrons had ceased as they turned their focus on Alex and her small group.

"I hate to interrupt," Perdita whispered, "but the dreaded mamas are watching. Might we sit and drink some lemonade?"

"An excellent idea, Miss Darby. I shall accompany you," Darlington offered, all politeness as he held out a hand to Perdita. She hesitated briefly, blushing as she finally put her arm through his. The moment Darlington had his back turned, Ambrose grasped Alex by the hand and tugged her closer to him, leaning his head down close to her ear. She glanced nervously about, but since Darlington had walked toward the lemonade tables, he and Alex were no longer as interesting to watch.

"Alex," he whispered, "that man is dangerous. Stay away from him. Do not let yourself be alone with him. He will ruin you."

Alex opened her mouth to speak but then nodded. There was a feral desperation in Ambrose's eyes and face that frightened her. If he, a hardened rakehell, was worried about a man like Darlington and his motives toward her, that was... She didn't know how to describe it, but a deep fear clawed at her insides, making her tense all over and a little light-headed. For the second time, she wondered if Ambrose knew exactly what the wager was in the betting books about her and if Darlington was somehow involved.

"Good." Ambrose relaxed a little. "Good," he repeated.

Perdita and Darlington were standing there, lemonade glasses in hand, watching them. Alex swallowed and tried to smile.

"Everything all right?" Darlington asked, his eyes moving between her and Ambrose.

"Of course," they replied in unison, which drew the attention of both Perdita and Darlington.

Her friend, always so astute, didn't miss Alex's silent warning glance and immediately distracted Darlington.

"How long will you be staying with us, Lord Darlington?" Perdita asked, raising her glass of lemonade and taking a sip. Of the four of them, Perdita appeared to be the most composed. Alex noticed Ambrose's wolfish expression and Lord Darlington's leonine relaxation, and she was confused.

Something wasn't right about Darlington's unexpected arrival, and she hadn't forgotten Ambrose's warning that she was in the betting books of a gentleman's club. That was never a good thing. But what could she do about it? Ladies had no control over what happened in clubs. Whatever was going on was more than just Ambrose being wary of Darlington over whatever might be in the betting books. The looks being exchanged between them —Ambrose's scowl and Darlington's amusement—felt too...personal. It unsettled her.

"I thought I might stay until I wore out my welcome," Darlington replied, still watching her and Ambrose.

"Then that might be a while. My mother is quite delighted you are staying with us." Perdita finished her lemonade and then glanced at Alex. "Alex, dear, I've a mind to get another glass. Wouldn't you like another?"

Alex stared down at her own still-full glass of lemonade, and both Ambrose and Darlington noticed, Ambrose with a frown and Darlington with a knowing smirk.

Alex let Perdita tug her to the lemonade table, and they bent their heads together.

"Lord Darlington's coming here was clearly not a coincidence," Perdita whispered.

"No, I fear not. Ambrose warned me to stay away from him, and I think..." Alex bit her lip before continuing. "I think that it's something to do with a wager in the betting books at one of the clubs in London."

"What?" Perdita hissed, her eyes wide in shock. "You are in a betting book?"

"Shh!" Alex warned her friend as a few ladies nearby looked their way.

"What sort of wager?" Perdita asked as she and Alex drew deeper into the gardens. Perdita was pale, and she licked her lips. "Alex, this isn't good that you're in the books. Do you have any idea of what the wager entails?"

"I don't know. Ambrose wouldn't tell me." Alex was startled by her friend's reaction. "What's the matter?"

Perdita's brows knit, her eyes far too serious, and it only made Alex's anxiety grow. "My brother, Thomas, he told me once about those books. Sometimes the bets are silly things, but other times they are quite serious. I'm afraid for you, Alex. If you're the subject of a bet, that cannot be good. Usually it means a man is betting on seducing you."

Alex swallowed hard. That would be a bad thing—a very bad thing. If men in London were plotting to ruin her, that was serious indeed. She'd heard of men going to great lengths to ruin ladies. There were always tales of desperate fortune hunters who talked young ladies into racing to Gretna Green to marry over the anvil against their families' protestations. But that wasn't all. She'd recently heard that a year ago a duke had abducted a young woman whose uncle had defrauded him over an investment scheme. The couple had thankfully ended up married, but the scandal had been all over London for months. Alex could imagine a man kidnapping a woman to win a wager if there was a large amount of money involved.

"You must get Mr. Worthing to tell you the particulars of the wager. We might be on better guard that way," Perdita suggested.

Ambrose hadn't wanted to tell her that much about the betting book earlier. Alex doubted she could convince Ambrose to do anything he did not wish to.

"Perdy, would you be able to distract Lord Darlington while he is here? I fear Lothbrook is too small a place, and whatever his intentions are, he might succeed whilst he is here." She knew she was asking a lot for her friend to risk her own ruination by keeping a known rogue distracted, but they had little choice.

"I can try. I'm sure Mama will help us—unknowingly, of course. She is quite smitten with the idea of a match between us."

"What?" That was news to Alex. "How do you know that?"

Her friend plucked a wildflower from the thick patch of blooms where an errant gardener had not taken care to remove them. Perdita played with the red petals and sighed.

"Mama wishes to buy me a husband, and a titled lord in desperate need of coin is easy prey. She will want to snatch him up for me. We've had chances before, but none of the other impoverished lords were..." Perdita blushed. "Well, Mama wants beautiful grandbabies, and she took one look at Lord Darlington and fainted. She will chase him for me if she gets a chance to convince him to marry me."

"Oh, Perdita." Alex's heart swelled with sympathy, and she hugged her friend. "You won't marry a man simply because your mother decrees it, will you?"

Perdita blinked, her eyes a little too bright. "I normally would say no, but...I confess, Lord Darlington is rather fascinating. He's the sort of man I might fall in love with, but I am not some chit just out of the schoolroom. He would break my heart if I dared to trust him with it. I honestly don't know what I would do if he proposed to me. I suppose I should be thankful he's more interested in you. But then again, he doesn't wish to marry you, likely only ruin you." She chuckled dryly. "Alex, dear, we are in quite a spot of bother, aren't we?"

"We are indeed." Alex raised her chin and glanced across the vast Darby gardens and found where Darlington and Ambrose stood talking.

"What if I went to London?" she said suddenly.

"London?" Perdita let the wildflower fall to the ground. "Why London?"

"Don't you see? I could hide in plain sight. Lord

Darlington has no chance of compromising me if we are in public all the time. I won't let my guard down for even a moment, and he won't have the chance to ruin me. My mother is there, and she could see that I'm never without a chaperone."

Her friend's eyes sharpened as she considered this new plan. "Yes, yes you are right. That might work."

Alex clasped her friend's hands in her own. "Would you come too, Perdy?"

"Why yes, of course," Perdita agreed. "There are a few places I wish to visit since it's been positively ages since I've been to London."

Alex grinned in the light. "Then we face London together." She knew that despite Perdita's mother wanting to marry her off, Perdita had avoided London as much as Alex had since they had come out in society. Neither of them had been interested in marrying simply to please others.

"Then it's settled." Perdita smiled back. "We flee to London." And they both dissolved in a fit of giggles.

❦

AMBROSE WATCHED ALEX AND PERDITA GIGGLING AND sharing conspiratorial glances at the far end of the garden. Vaughn Darlington stood beside him, brooding and silent.

How things had changed. Ambrose's chest tightened at

the thought. Years ago they would've been scheming together and stealing kisses from maids in the bushes.

"I suppose you've read the betting book at White's?" he asked.

They had seen each other the night the bet had been written down. Ambrose wouldn't forget watching Vaughn seated at a table only half a dozen feet from the betting book as Ambrose had listened to the low rumblings of the men discussing Alex's fate and her future ruination. At the time it had sickened him, and now, having met her, he was filled with righteous anger. A woman had a right to enjoy lovemaking and not be the subject of a man's cruelty. After what they'd shared in the garden, he knew she would be a good lover, and the thought of sharing her or giving her up to some brute from White's... He shook his head again, trying to erase thoughts of Alex outside the gardens with him above her and the glorious passion that he craved all for himself. Perhaps his reasons had become selfish, but he refused to let another man have her.

"I have seen the book."

"And you decided to take up the wager?" Ambrose asked carefully.

He had signed his name, officially taking on Alex's seduction himself, but it was still open for any man to beat him to it. It was that thought more than any other that was gnawing away at him. Not because he wanted to win for his own sake, but for Alex's.

"I might have." Vaughn was watching him rather than

the party guests. "And so have you, I believe." Then Vaughn looked toward Perdita and Alex. "Does she know you are playing her false to line your pockets?"

Rage bristled beneath Ambrose's skin. "See, this is why we are no longer friends. You assume I dictate my life choices based on my need for coin. But I'm not like you, Vaughn. I'm a friend of Lord Rockford's, and I accepted the bet to ensure that Alex's first time is enjoyable, not wretched as those others driven by money might make it. Unlike you, I have a heart."

Vaughn smiled. "So it's a noble cause for you, and I'm simply the *bastard* standing in your way? Well, may the best man win." Vaughn walked away, leaving Ambrose on edge.

He didn't want to be adversaries with his old friend, but things had changed. They'd once run through the fields, fishing poles in hand and singing bawdy songs on summer days. *And now we are enemies.* It left a bitter taste in his mouth. He stomped over to the lemonade tables and downed an entire glass in a few hasty gulps. It was rather ungentlemanly. A few matrons raised their brows and whispered behind their fans.

He offered an apologetic smile to the ladies before he headed for Alex. He didn't want to let her out of his sight. He caught a glimpse of Perdita and Alex approaching a small space in the garden where croquet had been set up for picnic guests. Alex was playfully swinging her mallet while Perdita was setting up the balls.

Ambrose was halfway to them when Vaughn beat him there.

"I'd love to join you ladies in a game," Vaughn said just as Ambrose reached them. Both Alex and her friend seem surprised.

"Well..." Alex started, but Ambrose spoke up.

"I wish to play as well. We could play doubles." He could be on Alex's team and keep her away from Vaughn.

"Splendid idea, Mr. Worthing," Alex said and tucked her arm through Perdita's. "We ladies shall play against you gentlemen, and I suspect we shall crow our victory over you." When Alex looked his way, her lips twitched impishly as though she'd guessed his intentions.

"Right," he grunted and retrieved a mallet. He simply kicked Vaughn's across the ground until it landed at the tip of the other man's leather shoes.

"Thank you." Vaughn's cold reply was dripping with sarcasm as he picked up the mallet.

"Perdita and I shall use the blue and black balls. You gentlemen may have the red and yellow." Alex escorted her friend away from the men to whisper again.

"This is not how I intended to spend my garden party," Ambrose muttered as he stole the red ball, leaving Vaughn the yellow one.

The ladies were allowed the first turn, because, well, because Ambrose was attempting to be a gentleman, after all. Alex was the first to strike the ball, and he couldn't help but admire the way the wind tugged at her skirts, the pale-blue muslin like a summer sky, the white lace at the edges of her hem and sleeves like wisps of clouds. Her hair was pulled back neatly with a few loose tendrils caressing her neck. It made him even hungrier for her, even after what they'd done in the garden earlier.

She'd opened herself up and let him see the real Alex, not the woman with a heart encased in iron. His Alex had been sweet, breathless, passionate, and a giving partner. He'd never imagined that. Too many ladies were afraid to touch a man back, to explore him. They believed they must lie still and wait until the man had sated himself, but that wasn't how lovemaking ought to be. Ambrose was a firm believer that a lady had as much right to her own passions and pleasures as any man did. Alex had been a perfect partner in pleasure. Someday she'd make a man a very happy husband.

The thought stopped him cold. The very idea of Alex with another man set his teeth on edge again.

It's not as though you could marry her, his inner voice reminded him. He didn't believe in tying himself to one woman for the rest of his life, nor did he have any interest in a country house filled to the brim with squalling babes and a fretful nanny. He preferred London and its wild pace and exciting venues.

Yet when he looked at Alex, standing proud and playful in the garden, wielding a croquet mallet, her hair blowing in the breeze and the heated blue sky that made her skin flushed and her eyes bright... Perhaps the country wasn't as very bad as all that.

In less than an hour, both he and Vaughn had been soundly beaten by their fair ladies, and in the midst of their defeat, he and Vaughn had been laughing and smiling. A twinge of pain in his chest made him long for days past, for friendships that had withered and died. He rubbed his chest above his heart as he watched Vaughn bending to pick up wickets with Miss Darby's assistance.

The girl was clearly interested in Vaughn, but he knew what obstacles Perdita faced, and Vaughn's cold heart was only part of her battle. The Darbys were a country-based family with no real influence in London and no titles. It was not hard for a gentleman like himself who had no title to become a favorite among the *ton*, but ladies without a blue-blooded lineage to boast of faced tough odds. Of course, if Vaughn was desperate enough, he would take any decent lady with any coin at the ready. Miss Darby didn't deserve to marry a bounder like Vaughn. She was too nice of a girl to be tricked into such a fate.

"Something troubles you?" Alex stood next to him, her face a picture of intense reflection, as though she was making a study of his thoughts.

He cleared his throat and gave a small nod in Perdita's direction. She was talking to Vaughn, her smile warm and her manner inviting but by no means coquettish. From what he had discerned of Alex's friend, Perdita had a generous and open heart. It made her perfect prey for a man like Vaughn.

"That troubles me. It bears watching." He didn't wish to elaborate, and thankfully Alex seemed to know his fears. She adjusted her white shawl about her shoulders. It had rosebuds embroidered along the hem, the blood-red petals drawing his eyes as he tried not to look at her face again. He was trapped in dreams of kissing her, plundering her sweet mouth and sliding his hands in the secret places of her body and swallowing her cries of ecstasy.

"And here I believed you were the man to scare us genteel ladies. But if Lord Darlington frightens even you, it is a concern I will keep in mind." Alex moved to stand in front of him, and he felt the heavy pull of her gaze. He raised his eyes, knowing he was damned.

"Ambrose..." She tilted her head as though sensing his reluctance.

When he locked his gaze on hers, he let out the words that would damn him.

"I cannot look at you without remembering the way it felt to hold you in my arms," he whispered huskily. "All I can think about is kissing you, the feel of you beneath me and drowning in your sweetness. It is torturing me." He didn't look away and neither did she, though her cheeks pinkened. It was a small mercy that the croquet field was a distance from the tea tables so they could not be overheard.

"If we were to start, we might never stop," she

murmured, her eyes fixed on his lips, with a wanton hungry expression that seemed to echo his own soul. They'd started down a dangerous road outside the gardens when they'd pleasured each other, and he knew it would soon deepen when they finally made love. *Made love.* He'd never really used those words when thinking of bedding a woman, but with Alex, there had been a softness in his heart that frightened him.

Lord, he was damned for wanting her.

9

There was no way he could resist kissing Alex once they started. She was temptation wrapped in sin like no other woman had been for him before.

"If we were to start, we might never stop...and I shouldn't want to—not with you," Alex confessed in a whisper. They were standing so close he could feel the heat of her, and he hated that they weren't somewhere he could secrete her away and kiss her in the way they wanted.

"Am I so wicked, Alex?" His voice sounded a little deep and throaty, and her eyes darkened. He couldn't help but continue. "Do you see me as a phantom who would steal into your bed after darkness falls and ravish you?" The mere idea had his body hardening with arousal. She was staring at him hungrily, as though she was picturing the same thing he was.

"You are wicked indeed," she replied breathlessly, "because I would be tempted to leave the door unlocked..."

Leave the door unlocked? Was that an invitation? Good God. The short distance between them was charged with such tension that he was afraid if either of them moved, it would create sparks. In that moment, nothing existed outside of being with Alex. They were in their own secluded world, filled with heated breaths and promises glinting in their eyes and at the corners of their smiles.

"Alex, love!" her father's voice boomed, making Ambrose jump. Lord Rockford was striding toward them, beaming.

"I just heard that your cousin Rachel will be joining us for supper tonight. She brought the children. I thought you might be glad to see them." Rockford was grinning, and it was clear that Rockford adored children. He had no grandbabies, and once Alex's reputation lay in tatters on the altar of society's gossipers, she might never find a husband, at least not a good one. And knowing Alex, she would rather embrace spinsterhood than settle for a man she didn't love.

And I'm the bloody bastard who will shatter those dreams when I ruin her.

He had no choice. Some man was going to get Alex and destroy her, and better that it be a man who cared about her than one who didn't. But that didn't erase the heavy weight on his chest at the thought of being responsible for this. He would ruin two lives, Alex's and Rockford's.

"I should get home and see that the cook knows to prepare extra places for supper," Alex said, her smile infectious as she glanced between Ambrose and her father.

"Good idea. I'd come home with you, but Mrs. Darby has enlisted me in a croquet match. Damned if I know how to tell that woman no to anything," Rockford chuckled. "So that brings me to a request, Ambrose. Would you mind escorting my daughter home?" Rockford asked.

"Of course, it would be my pleasure." Ambrose was relieved and excited at the idea of catching a few minutes alone with Alex, but he didn't look her way lest he betray his thoughts or his excitement in front of her father.

"Let me make my excuses to Miss Darby, and then we shall leave." Alex left to find their hostess, and Ambrose stood by Rockford.

"Miss Rockford has a cousin?" Ambrose asked.

The earl grinned. "Rachel. She and Alex are very close, almost like sisters. She is the daughter of my wife's elder sister. Rachel married a nice gentleman from Sussex. They don't visit often enough. You'll like her husband. Mr. Brandon is a good man."

"I look forward to making their acquaintance." Ambrose meant it. He was curious to meet a woman Alex was close to aside from Perdita, although he wasn't sure why exactly. But he wanted to know more about her, this beauty who hid herself away in the country.

Alex came back a moment later and looked at Ambrose. "I'm ready."

She collected her shawl and her bonnet and looked eager to leave. Beyond her stood Vaughn, just at the edge of the croquet field, scowling slightly. He had to remain behind since he was officially a guest of the Darbys and not the Rockfords. Ambrose couldn't help but flash him a smug smile, which made the other man turn his back and try to wave off the crowds of ladies around the tea tables.

Ambrose offered Alex his arm, and they walked away from Darby House and toward the Rockford estate.

"Today was rather wonderful." Alex sighed dreamily. "It was quite perfect."

"I have to agree. I was woken up far too early, had to dine on salty porridge, was lost in a cow field where I almost fell on my arse when I slipped in cow dung, and was soundly beaten at croquet by two ladies. Yes, absolutely splendid day." He grinned at her cheekily. "Aside from that, everything else about today has been rather wonderful, especially kissing you senseless." This time he let his tone turn husky as he spoke. He wanted her to remember every kiss as vividly as he did.

He thought of when he'd pleasured her in a secluded part of the gardens, making her moan his name, and how he'd wanted to lie there forever with her in the warm grass and listen to the hum of bees and the chatter of birds.

And then when they'd played croquet and she'd made him laugh at her excitement over beating him soundly. He was usually competitive, but her winning fairly had him strangely full of quiet joy. There was something in the way her eyes had sparkled and her lips had curved into an honest smile.

"Although I'm still cross with you for sending me to a field of cows," he added, chuckling.

"I couldn't resist." She bit her lip, but he saw how she was smiling. "I couldn't let a known rake stay under my roof without attempting to drive you away. It's what any decent lady would do."

They entered the road and left the houses and picnic behind. It was a perfect moment for him to have her back in his arms, even for a brief moment, without the watchful eyes of Lothbrook's matrons and gentlemen to see. Ambrose stopped them, and she turned to face him. "And now? Will you still try to push me away?" he asked. *Please say no...* It was fun to chase a woman who resisted, but he wanted no resistance from Alex, only mutual desire, because wanting to be with her was becoming less and less of a game to him every minute he spent with her.

"Now..." Her gaze was cloudy with confusion. "I won't deny that while you frustrate me to no end, I like you... and I like what we did in the gardens." This last was uttered in a blushing whisper.

"But..."

He could sense she was hesitating about something.

"What are we doing, Ambrose? This—the kisses, the gardens, and the rest?"

His eager smile faded as he knew what she was asking. There would be no proposal, no declarations of love, and she deserved that, yet he couldn't give it to her. He was not a man to marry, no matter how tempting the thought of Alex was. He didn't trust his heart to be loyal. He'd never been able to focus on just one woman, and he would not be a husband who left his wife's bed. Better to not be a husband at all than to be disloyal.

"Alex, sweetheart, I don't know." He cupped her face, gazing deeply into her eyes. "I only know that right now, I'd go mad without kissing you."

Her breath hitched and her lashes fluttered. It was an invitation he couldn't resist. When their lips met, the kiss was soft and hot, burning him up slowly from the inside out. How could one kiss be so damned good? Like drinking a glass of warm brandy by the fire while it snowed outside. He dined upon her lips, tasting her sweetness and reveling in the way she curled her arms around his neck to keep them close. It was a long while before they broke apart and had to catch their breath.

"Alex, I don't know what the future holds, but let's take it one day, one kiss at a time."

Alex nibbled her bottom lip and sighed. "One day at a time." She nodded to herself and then straightened her shoulders. "We must get back to the house."

They started walking again, and Ambrose's heart was

strangely heavy. He didn't like the sad, distant look in her eyes. He wanted Alex right there in that moment with him, not miles away. Tonight he would come to her, reclaim her attention and her heart for as long as he could.

"RACHEL!" ALEX RUSHED TO GREET HER COUSIN. RACHEL laughed and hugged her fiercely.

"I've missed you," Alex murmured, her eyes burning with tears. Sussex was too far away, and she missed her cousin dearly. They'd been as close as sisters once, before marriage and babes had separated them by time and distance.

Her cousin smiled, and then whatever they might have said was interrupted by the tugging of tiny hands on Alex's skirts.

"Aunt Alex?" A cherubic little girl of five years was looking up at her with wide cornflower-blue eyes.

"Emma!" Alex bent and lifted the girl into her arms. "My goodness, you've grown." The little girl smiled and clapped her hands.

"And Griffin, where is he?" Alex asked, searching for signs of Rachel's three-year-old boy.

"Here," a loud, cheery voice boomed. Randolph Brandon came in the front door, a tiny boy in his arms.

"Randolph!" Alex hugged him as well before kissing little Griffin's cheek. The boy squirmed and rubbed at his face, scowling in the way little boys always did when they pretended not to enjoy receiving kisses. Randolph set the boy down, and he trundled on chubby legs over to where Ambrose stood, hanging at the edge of the room as though unsure whether he was part of the gathering.

"Hello," the little boy chirped, tugging at Ambrose's trouser leg.

"Er... hello..." Ambrose greeted the little boy, and Alex couldn't help but giggle at Ambrose's perplexed expression. He clearly didn't spend much time around children, and had no idea how to act. Alex shared an amused glance with Rachel as Randolph exchanged introductions with Ambrose.

"Come, Alex, we must catch up." Rachel's green eyes were bright with mischief as they walked out of the entryway into the drawing room. The green-satin-walled drawing room was warm with the glow of the freshly- lit fire in the white marble fireplace. Alex led her cousin and little Emma to a settee. Emma settled herself firmly between her mother and her aunt, swinging her little booted feet, her tiny delicate hands folded in her lap.

"Well now, Alex. Who is that enchanting fellow talking to my husband?" Her cousin's tone was full of teasing and curiosity.

"That is Mr. Worthing. He is the son of one of Father's old friends, and apparently Father has known him since he was a child."

Rachel played with her elbow-length gloves, her

assessing gaze taking in Ambrose's expensively tailored clothes and his fine physique.

"And he came to visit you from London?" she asked.

"Not exactly. He came to renew his acquaintance with my father. We'd never met before."

"Is that so?" Rachel looked between her and Ambrose. Little Emma imitated her mother's quizzical, analytical gaze, and Alex almost laughed. The child was growing up too fast.

"It isn't like that, Rachel."

"Oh? I thought perhaps that you'd found someone new, after Marshall..." She trailed off, and Alex winced at the little twinge of pain in her chest. She didn't want to think about Marshall or how his betrayal of her young, foolish heart had hurt her so deeply. Those types of wounds didn't simply heal overnight. They lingered, like a bad cough in the middle of winter, leaving one uncomfortable and feeling dreadful for months.

"My dear, I'm sorry. I shouldn't have mentioned Marshall. It's just..."

"Just what?" Alex asked.

"Mr. Worthing hasn't taken his eyes off you since we arrived, and well, a man doesn't pay such a marked interest in a woman unless he's truly smitten."

Both Alex and Rachel glanced Ambrose's way, and to Alex's delight, she saw him showing his pocket watch to Griffin. The little boy was reaching out to touch the golden watch face when Ambrose pretended to shut the lid on his fingers and the boy shrieked in delight at the game. It was just as Rachel had pointed out—every few seconds, Ambrose's gaze darted to her, then his cheeks reddened slightly, and he focused back on the toddler.

"How do you know?" she asked.

Her cousin smiled. "It was that way with Randolph. We met in the middle of a ball, and he couldn't stop looking at me. I was flattered, naturally, but I was used to men looking my way since my debut. But when he tripped in the middle of a quadrille and sent an entire line of men falling down in the middle of the assembly room because he was watching me and not his feet...well...I knew it was more than simple attraction." Rachel's lips curved. "Sometimes two people are simply drawn to each other so strongly that it cannot be denied or fought against, only surrendered to."

"Surrendered to?" Alex was listening raptly to her cousin, her heart beating fast and hard.

"Love is just that, surrendering, not fighting. When you want to be with someone, you must give up part of yourself forever to that other person and he to you. It's a fair exchange of hearts and souls."

"You and Randolph truly knew that early that you were meant to be?"

"Yes, we knew, but it wasn't something I could explain. There was no divine lightning or choir of angels heralding it as our destiny. It came softly, almost slowly, a need to see each other, to hear each other speak, to whisper in the dark and to dance. Lust came first, as it often does, but even lust tempers over time, and when it does, you're left with the sweetest, most tender passion of all. The passion of the heart."

Alex's throat constricted and she tried to swallow. Thinking of that sort of love, something so powerful, so all-encompassing, was strangely frightening, and yet she wanted it, wanted it so much it brought tears to her eyes.

Was Rachel right? Was Ambrose smitten with her? Alex was too afraid to hope that she was right. As much as Alex didn't want to admit it, she liked Ambrose, *more* than liked him, and realizing that made her feel weak and vulnerable. It was so much safer not to fall in love, and she feared she was already falling. There might be no going back from where she was. What if it happened all over again? What if she opened her heart to him, let him inside that vulnerable spot, and he wounded her? Could she survive another blow to her heart?

"Dinner should be ready," her father announced. "Rachel, I've had the footman set up two places for the children."

"Thank you, Uncle." Rachel smiled with delight and gave Alex's hand a gentle squeeze in silent support.

Everyone walked toward the dining room, Rachel and her husband going first to see to the children. Ambrose sidled up behind Alex. She was intimately aware of his body heat, and the feel of him so close made her dizzy.

"The children are to dine with us?" he asked in a low

whisper, close enough that it stirred the fine hairs behind her left ear, making her shiver. She didn't miss the note of surprise in his voice.

She turned her head to reply and blinked at how close they were. He placed a hand on her lower back as they exited the drawing room. Her gown was not particularly thin, but the heat of his palm seemed to sink through the layers of fabric with a delicious burn.

"I know it's unusual, but Papa loves the children. The idea of shutting them away in a dusty old nursery offends him."

"Ah." Ambrose's lips twitched. "Such a soft heart, your father."

"Yes, he is," she agreed, smiling back, but another twinge of pain hit her at the thought of how sad her father must be to have no grandbabies of his own. She was an only child, and she'd failed to give him that one great joy. Had she been too selfish all these years in hiding away? It was entirely possible she might have found a decent man to marry, one who would love her and tolerate her bluestocking tendencies and her love of the country, but there would be no passion. She couldn't fathom being married to someone and not feeling that wild desperation that made her heart sing and her skin flush. As always, though, she questioned whether she was falling into a trap where only lust drove her and not love.

But I haven't lusted after anyone since Marshall...except for Ambrose.

"Alex?" Ambrose whispered, studying her face closely. More than ever, in that moment she wanted to lean into him and take comfort in being in his arms. That was one of the many dangerous things about Ambrose—he made her *long* for him. Even in such a simple way as to be held and comforted.

"It's nothing," she lied, forcing a bright smile upon her face and stepping away from him as they entered the dining room.

The footmen were seating Emma and Griffin between their parents. The little girl was daintily folding her linen napkin on her lap, watching her mother closely. Griffin, however, was bouncing up and down in his seat, making little *whoosh* noises, which amused Randolph even as he tried to shush the boy.

"This should be most entertaining," Ambrose chuckled as he led Alex to a seat opposite her cousin and pulled back her chair. She murmured a polite thanks and then tensed as he sat down beside her. It was so strange to have him here at an intimate family dinner, yet as the courses were served and conversation began, Ambrose simply fit into her family as though he'd always been a part of it. Her chest was filled with a fuzzy warmth that made her unable to stop smiling.

"So, Worthing, you spend much of your time in London?" Randolph asked.

"Yes, I like the liveliness of the city." He paused, then

glanced Alex. "But the country is proving to have its charms."

Randolph smiled, his brown eyes twinkling. "That it does. A man never realizes how full life is in the country until he's happily settled down in a nice house with a garden and acreage to go shooting in. Nothing compares to it."

"I quite agree. There's a peacefulness here that I hadn't thought I'd enjoy so much. The gardens are quite pleasant." His lips twitched as he sipped his wine from his crystal goblet.

A heavy blush stole over Alex's face as she knew what he was referring to. Their garden tryst during the picnic and how they'd both been carried away. It had indeed been very pleasant—more than pleasant.

Suddenly Griffin used his spoon to fling a giant spoonful of peas straight across the table at Alex and Ambrose. The little green projectiles sprayed wide, plinking into water glasses and bouncing off their clothes.

For a second no one spoke or reacted, except for one of the young footmen hiding in the corner who stifled a chuckle behind a gloved hand. He hastily recovered himself and straightened, his eyes focused straight ahead.

"Griffin! You eat peas, you do not toss them at family members!" Rachel chastised sharply, looking completely horrified at her son's wayward behavior. "Mr. Worthing, please accept my apologies —"

Griffin's bottom lip began to quiver as his mother

scowled darkly at him with motherly vengeance gleaming in her eyes.

"Nonsense." Ambrose burst out laughing. "The little fellow has quite good aim." He winked at the little boy. Seeing Ambrose's conspiratorial wink, the boy brightened, even under his mother's now -embarrassed glare.

"Randolph, dear, I think it might be time to put the children to bed. They can finish their supper in the nursery." Rachel shot her husband a determined look.

"Yes, yes, of course, my love." Randolph scooped up Griffin and took Emma's hand and hastily exited the dining room. Her father watched them go, a wistful expression on his face.

"Such little dears," he murmured. "That Griffin is delightfully cheeky, isn't he?"

"Too much like his father," Rachel said with a sigh, but her lips were curved upward.

Alex's gaze dropped to her plate, a sinking feeling in her stomach. She really had disappointed her father by not marrying and having children. It was painfully obvious how much he longed for them.

"Well"—Rockford cleared his throat and looked around—"shall we retire to the drawing room? Ladies, I assume you have much to discuss. Ambrose and I will drink some port in my study before we join you, won't we, my boy?"

"Of course," Ambrose agreed amicably.

The gentlemen escorted them to the drawing room before they left on their quest for port and cigars.

A footman brought a set of sherry glasses to the ladies on a silver tray. Alex accepted her glass of sherry and took a sip before turning to her cousin. They finally had a chance to speak alone without anyone overhearing.

"Are you and Randolph headed to London?"

Rachel nodded as she settled into her chair by the fire. "Yes, we have a few dinners to attend, and then we return to Sussex. We don't like the children to be in the city for too long. There's so much pressure to grow up there. In the country, they can chase dogs down the lane and ride horses and swim in the pond behind the house."

"Emma seems determined to grow up," Alex observed.

Her cousin nodded, her eyes sad. "She is, takes after me too much I think, just as Griffin is so like Randolph, always getting into scrapes."

They both sipped their sherry, the grandfather clock in the corner ticking away into the silence. Alex had to speak to her, to get advice from one of the few people aside from Perdita whom she trusted.

"I'm so glad you came, Rachel. Truly," Alex whispered, her voice suddenly catching.

"Alex, dear, what's the matter?" Her cousin rose from her chair and came to her, hugging her.

"I'm afraid I've been very silly—very silly indeed. I wish you hadn't left..."

Rachel had helped her pick up the pieces of her heart when Marshall had married someone else.

"What have you done that is silly?" Rachel asked, her eyes full of worry.

"It's Ambrose—I mean, Mr. Worthing. I'm afraid I've l let him become too close to me." She wasn't sure how to say it, that she'd been too free with her body and her desires.

"I see," Rachel replied. There was no judgment in her face, but rather a deep understanding.

"I'm afraid I'll always be alone, that this might be the one chance I have to know what life and love are before he goes back to London. Is that terrible of me?"

Her cousin's green eyes were soft, like summer grass covered in a morning fog.

"No, it isn't terrible. You have every right to want to know the joys of being in love and expressing that love, but you must take care. If you were to get in the family way, it would be..." She trailed off, but Alex understood.

It would be the end of the already small social life that she had in Lothbrook. If she had a babe, she would want to keep it, which meant she would not be able to stay in a town that knew the truth of her disgrace. She would be exiled to some distant part of the country with relatives she barely knew, in a town with no friends.

"Have you and Mr. Worthing been fully intimate?"

Alex shook her head. They had come close, but not yet.

Her cousin pursed her lips before speaking again. "If you do wish for full intimacy, you must demand that he take care. He should know what that means. There are things he could do to prevent you from being with child."

"I feel so trapped, Rachel," she confessed. "I avoid London because of Marshall, and yet I don't feel I can breathe here sometimes. I just want...some small measure of happiness. Is that so wrong?" She wanted to confess about the wager in the betting books and that she was planning to flee to London to escape Lord Darlington, but something made her hold that inside. She didn't want to worry Rachel, even though she valued her cousin's counsel.

"No, of course not. Perhaps Mr. Worthing will be the answer. I see the way he looks at you, and I don't believe you should take his interest so lightly. He let your nephew throw peas in his face. That tells me much of what sort of man he is and that he will endure much to be with you."

Alex was too afraid to hope her cousin was right. She'd let a man break her heart once before, and it had almost destroyed her. Could she let that happen again? Was it already too late?

❧ 10 ❧

Long after the household had settled into their beds for the night, Alex lay awake in her bed, watching the firelight from her small hearth create shadows on the baroque red satin- covered walls. The evening had turned chilly, and the house was hushed save for the occasional soft sound that echoed down the corridor. She listened to the house creak and shift as night wore on, and at last, she heard the sound she hoped for and yet dreaded. Light steps outside her door. The twist of the door handle...

She sat up and watched the door open as Ambrose slipped into her chamber. The sound of the door closing was quiet, but it seemed to echo through the room. For a long moment, he simply stood there, staring at her, his handsome features a mysterious mask. She could almost feel his gaze on her, the focus and intensity of his eyes, and it made her shiver.

Her heart pounded and she clutched her coverlet to her chest, strangely afraid, but not of him. She was going to take that last step to ruination tonight. She was going to let him come to her bed. It was usual to be a little frightened, wasn't it? She knew what to expect; she'd had her mother explain the particulars of men and women coming together during her first season. Since then she'd heard enough of other ladies whispering, not to mention that encounter in the gardens today had been a thorough education.

"Alex," he murmured, the firelight making his eyes glow, and her name was a quiet question.

It warmed her to know he wouldn't push her, wouldn't force her to do anything she didn't wish. The hungry light in his eyes was tempered with gentleness, a preparedness to leave if she told him to. That made all the difference in the world, because she did want him, desperately, possibly even more than he wanted her.

"Lock the door behind you," she whispered, her body suddenly tense. She was doing this, she was going to become a ruined woman, but no one would know what they'd do tonight. Just the two of them...in the quiet...in the dark. An excited shiver rippled through her.

He latched the door and walked over to the bed. He unbuttoned his vest slowly, and she watched his long, elegant fingers slipping buttons through their slits before he shrugged the finely embroidered waistcoat to the floor. She glanced down at it, studying the firelight making the gold threading that formed a pair of stags in the woods glow. It was beautiful, like him. Many men would have patterns sewn into their clothes, but he'd chosen a scene, two bucks facing each other across a stretch of woods completed in varying tones of silver and gold.

"I..." She slid to the edge of the bed, her nerves on edge and her stomach assailed with fluttering butterflies. She reached up to help him pull his shirt out of his buckskin trousers as he lifted it over his head, baring his chest. Her palms settled on his skin, tentative at first. He watched her, unspeaking, unmoving as she trailed her fingers over his body. It was fascinating to touch a man's bare chest, feel the power of his muscles, and explore his dusky nipples. The hollow of his throat...and the dark line of hair that trailed from his navel down to below his trousers. She reached for the front of his pants.

"We don't have to do this if you aren't ready." He laid his hands over hers against his trousers, stilling their trembling. She peeped up at him through her gold-brown lashes.

"That's not what a rake is supposed to say to a woman's he's planning to deflower."

Ambrose gazed down at her, no smile, no charm, just sincerity. "This isn't about that. I don't want it to be just... I don't want to be just some rake to you. I just want it to be you and me here in this bed tonight. No games, no lies, no thoughts of tomorrow." He seemed so serious, so earnest that she believed him.

"Just us?"

He nodded and lifted his hands to cup her face so he could lean down and kiss her. It was a wicked kiss with a slip of tongue. Yet he made it a kiss full of sweetness. He dropped his hands, still kissing her. She reached for the front of his trousers again. He shed his pants, and she scooted back on the bed as he climbed in with her. Her bed wasn't small, but sharing it with someone—a very big, masculine someone—made it nice, cozy.

Ambrose leaned over her, smiling as he brushed her hair back from her face. He stared at her for a long moment, his gaze soft and his sensual mouth curved in a tender smile. Everything inside her stilled as she brushed his hair out of his eyes and smiled back at him. This was right—this felt wonderful. Just the two of them in her bed, the fire crackling and their quiet shared breaths as they were readying to embark on a journey that seemed written in their hearts long before they'd ever shared that first waltz.

Ambrose licked his lips. "Lord, you are beautiful. Truly beautiful."

"Would you help me out of my nightgown?" she asked.

He grinned as he let her sit up a little, and they pulled her long white nightgown up and away. It floated to the floor in a heap of white lace. Alex held her breath as she sat completely bare before him. Her breasts rose and fell with her beating heart, and she tensed as he cupped one breast. His large hand was gentle as he lifted it and brushed the pad of his thumb over one peak. It felt exquisite, his hands exploring her.

"Lie back for me," he encouraged as she slid down on the bed. "We must be quiet so as not to be overhead."

He leaned over her again, kissing her lips, her chin, and her throat. His mouth moved lower, to her collarbone, and then he finally nuzzled one breast before he took her nipple between his lips, sucking gently. The erotic tug went straight to her womb, making her womb clench and her thighs quiver. She reacted instinctively, sliding her fingers through his hair, gripping his head as he teased her breast, and then he lifted his head, flashing her a grin as he slid farther down her body, parting her thighs. Alex tried to close her legs, but he used his hands to keep them braced apart. He placed more soft hot kisses to her lower belly, the top of her mound, and—

"Oh!" She inhaled sharply as he licked her slick folds. The rasping feel of his tongue in such a sensitive secret place was too much. Her body quivered with spasms, like an arrow unleashed from a tight bowstring. She let go, and a climax rolled through her. His mouth felt infinitely more sinful than his fingers had.

"Like that, do you?" he teased softly.

"Yes...very much." She wriggled languidly as he settled into the cradle of her thighs.

"Good, I did as well. Your taste is exquisite." He licked

his lips again, and then he shifted his body, and she felt his hard shaft nudge her. Here it was—the moment that would change her life forever, and possibly his, she hoped. There could be no going back, and it was frightening, but her desire to be with him like this outweighed that fear. Their eyes sought each other's, and she watched a rapid play of emotions she couldn't quite recognize flit across his face.

Ambrose didn't ask for her permission, but he waited, their gazes locked. She gave him a tiny nod. He kissed her greedily, his lips rough, while the rest of him was infinitely tender. He pushed into her, stretching her. There was a twist, a hard thrust, and a sharp inner pain. Alex whimpered and then bit his lip, but he didn't stop kissing her. Long moments later, they began to move, their bodies sliding in the dark, the sheets falling to their hips as Ambrose made love to her.

Each time he entered her, the glorious fullness was overwhelming, but she hungered for it again and again. Her nails dug into his back and his shoulders as she clung to him. He rode her slowly at first, their bodies seeking a natural rhythm that she made quicker by using her hips to drag him deeper into her. Her breathing was shallow, and she felt her body racing faster, higher, toward some infinite height of true pleasure. Ambrose's gaze was hungry and his lips ravenous as he kissed every inch of her upper body. His hips jerked harder, and she clenched down around him inside her.

When he growled low, the sound vibrated through her and it was too much, too good. He pounded faster. The sound of their slick bodies coming together and their ragged breaths made her fall off the edge. Another climax exploded through her, and her vision was spotted with white stars. He cried out, and she kissed him to silence the sound as he came apart above her. In that moment, she knew she loved him. How could she not? The vulnerable truth of his own emotions was shining in his eyes as he found his pleasure with her.

They lay together, bodies still joined, sharing breaths and secret smiles until the fire had died and the night was in full bloom. Alex felt exposed and vulnerable, yet she wasn't alone—he was with her. His body was wrapped around hers, easing away all her fears.

"Stay with me," Alex begged, stroking the arm around her waist. He was holding on to her from behind as they lay on their sides, bodies pressed together perfectly like a pair of spoons nestled in a drawer.

Ambrose nuzzled her ear, placing a soft kiss there. "There's no place I wish to be but here."

"Good," she murmured and was ready to drift off to sleep when she suddenly tensed. "Ambrose?" Her voice vibrated with new fear.

"What is it, love?" he asked, his voice a low rumble.

"Did you...take precautions? I forgot to ask you to." She'd been so foolishly obsessed with him in her bed that she'd forgotten her cousin's advice.

"I..." He sighed wearily. "I regret I did not. I knew better, but the moment you touched me I went up in bloody flames." He kissed her shoulder. "But it's unlikely you will find yourself with child the first time after you make love."

"But if I should..."

"Then we face that consequence together," he replied.

Consequence...the word seemed so dreaded, so heavy and unwanted. But would a child born between them be a consequence or a blessing?

"Be at ease, my love, please. I can almost hear your thoughts pounding in your head. I promise you I will take care of you should a babe result from tonight."

Alex turned a little in his arms. "Do you want children? I mean not now, but perhaps someday?" Until she'd seen her father around Griffin and Emma, she hadn't thought much of babies. Now she realized it would be nice someday to have a child.

He smiled a little, almost shyly. "Before today I would have said no. But a little mite throwing peas across the dinner table was much more entertaining than I had anticipated. It might be fun to have some little ones running about my house." His tone was full of amusement and surprise.

His mind had been changed tonight, she could tell, and something about that gave her hope to dream. Because the moment they'd shared that first passionate embrace in the garden, she'd realized that she wanted to think of a future with him, even as foolish as it was to dream of marrying a rakehell.

"Alex, will you tell me what makes you afraid of London?" he asked.

She shivered in his arms. "I don't want to talk about it."

He sighed softly, the sound sad and sweet. "Talking about it might help. I want you to know you can be honest with me."

"And would you be honest with me?" she countered, scrutinizing his features for any hint of an attempt to deceive her.

He nodded. "Ask me anything."

"You and Lord Darlington...there's a history there. What is it?"

"We were friends once. Close friends." Ambrose trailed his fingertips along her arm, the touch soothing and sweetly sensual.

"What happened between you? It was obvious you weren't on good terms." Alex was surprised but delighted that he was talking to her.

"It was several years ago, but his parents died and he inherited the title of Viscount Darlington, and he inherited his father's debts as well. That changed him. He didn't want any charity that I or our other friend Gareth could provide. He wanted to support himself, but he started breaking me at the gaming tables, even though it wasn't enough to sustain him. His father had bankrupted the estate, and Vaughn was holding on to his family's holdings by the skin of his teeth."

"And you didn't agree with his method of surviving?" she guessed.

"No, I didn't. And our friendship was the casualty of that war."

"I'm sorry," she whispered.

"Things happen. Friends grow apart," he muttered and looked away from her for a moment, his gaze melancholy and distant.

"Ambrose." She gently tugged his face down to hers and kissed him. He returned the kiss, but it was gentle and full of a softer passion, one that didn't need to end up with them making love. For some reason that made her heart turn over, and she snuggled closer to him.

"Will you tell me about London now?" he asked.

The tender moment seemed to fade slightly as she realized she would have to tell him.

"I...was in love once, long ago. The man and I had an understanding, but he left for London right before my debut and married a wealthy heiress. When it came time for my presentation and my coming out, I simply couldn't face the *ton*. I couldn't face him and his wife and see them together. It hurt too much." There, she's said it. Maybe he wouldn't ask her anything else.

His fingers traced her jaw, and his eyes were soft as he gazed down at her. "Whoever that man was, he is a fool. I could not think of any reason to leave you, if you were mine." This time he kissed her, and his lips burned, scorching a path from her mouth to her throat, then to her collarbone. It was a long while before they were sated and lying quiet again. He'd made her forget about her heartache and reminded her that life could still offer some joys even to those healing from broken hearts.

"Go to sleep, my love." He pressed a kiss to her cheek.

Alex closed her eyes, pushed back against him. If only they never had to leave this room or this bed. She let the darkness of sleep overtake her. Tomorrow she would have to face the consequences of tonight.

Tomorrow...

AMBROSE HELD ALEX IN HIS ARMS AND TRIED TO process the flood of emotions he was experiencing. He had slept with dozens of women over the last several years and but rarely had mistresses. He loved the thrill of the chase, the seduction, and the catch. Then he walked away. He didn't like forming close, lasting relationships with women. Yet all those other nights of passion with strangers felt empty and hollow compared to the golden glow of making love to Alex.

From the moment he'd stepped into her bedchamber, he'd felt the beating pulse of attraction and something more. It was a purer sense of connection, something he'd never felt with any woman before. She had been bold and brave yet full of innocence. He'd enjoyed introducing her to passion and exploring her body. It was so much more than sex. Kissing her had been as vital as drawing his next breath. And when he'd possessed her, her tight sheath gripping him like a fist, it hadn't been a simple physical pleasure. He had felt like he was flying, and she'd been with him. For the first time, intercourse had been a moment to share, not to enjoy on his own. In the past, he always made sure his lovers found pleasure as well, but it had never felt like something he'd done together with them.

I used them as they used me.

It wasn't that way with Alex. With her, it had been about mutual, shared joy, and it had been about being with her and sharing himself with her.

And she'd asked him to stay. He would not have dared to stay with previous lovers, nor would he have wanted to. But holding Alex as she slept, their bodies pressed skin to skin, he couldn't imagine any other place in the world that he'd rather be in that moment. Making love to this woman had been sweeter than his first kiss. It had been more thrilling than racing his horse through the fields as he hunted. It was more than everything that had once given him pleasure in life.

I'm falling for this woman, a feisty country girl who can't stand London, and I'm destined to ruin her and break her heart in order to save her.

Fate was a cruel wench who was dealing him a terrible

hand at the celestial gaming tables. He couldn't help but wonder if this was how his friend Gareth had felt when he'd met Helen. He hadn't thought his friend could ever love again after his first wife died in childbirth, yet he had. *Am I to going to fall in love? And at what cost? I have only a black heart to give this woman. And she won't want me when I've ruined her in every way.* He stared down at her face, marveling at how she could rest so peacefully. He couldn't shake the guilt that ate at his gut and made him sick.

Damn whoever wrote the bet down in that book at White's. They would destroy a sweet, wonderful woman for the sake of their own amusement. *And damn me for being the fool to try to save her by ruining her.*

He buried his face in her neck, inhaling her sweet scent and trying not to think about what the morning would bring.

11

"London? But I thought you didn't like the city?" Ambrose watched Alex pace the floor of the drawing room. Her pale-pink muslin gown whispered along the carpets as she walked. After last night, he'd believed their night of passion would have drawn them closer, but come the morning, Alex had seemed worried and withdrawn. Now he understood. She was contemplating going to London, a place he knew she didn't like.

"You said Lord Darlington was dangerous. I don't believe the country is a good place to stay while he is around."

"Fair enough," Ambrose sighed. "It would be easier for him to get to you out here." It would be even easier in London for her to fall prey to the other men wanting to win the wager. It put her in danger no matter where she was.

I should just lock her away in a bloody tower and be done with it.

"So Perdita and I shall go to London. I thought I might visit your sister. If you are willing to offer us a proper introduction?" Her words were casual, but he sensed she was quite serious about meeting his sister.

Alex stopped pacing and was staring at him, her eyes full of hope.

"Yes, of course. Violet would love that. I shall accompany you ladies in the coach, of course." There was no chance he'd let her go off on her own to London. He'd be with her every step of the way so he could ensure her safety.

"What?" Alex replied in surprise. "There's no need to accompany us." She blushed as he crossed the distance and gripped her waist gently.

"Are you that ready to be rid of me after last night?" His voice came out a throaty whisper, rumbling as he remembered everything that they had shared last night. Part of him worried that she might not have felt as overwhelmed as he had in bed the previous night. Last night he'd believed she was as wrapped up in their intimacy as he was, but perhaps he'd been wrong. The thought of her not being as obsessed and fascinated with him as he was with her was like a blow to his stomach.

"No, it isn't that." She smiled shyly. "I just didn't want

to make you feel obligated to do something you did not wish to do." Her words quieted the fears that had been racing through him, and he smiled at her, loving how her blush only deepened. If there hadn't been a small chance of her father or a servant walking in on them, he would have kissed the woman senseless.

"There's nothing I wish to do more than escort you to London and introduce you to my sister." And he meant it. A trip to London would require a stop at an inn, another chance to be alone with her before he had to ruin her reputation and her life. He winced at the thought.

"Everything all right?" she asked.

"Hmm? Oh yes, just thinking, that's all." He grinned and leaned in to steal a quick kiss. There were plans to be made, and he wanted to get her to London to meet his sister. "We should pack and leave if we wish to reach a decent inn for dinner. I can send a boy ahead and reserve a set of rooms."

"That would be wonderful, thank you. I'll need additional lodging for my maid and Perdita's." She didn't seem to mind at all that he had taken charge of the situation. His headstrong Alex had the good sense to listen to him.

Ambrose nodded. "Of course."

"Oh, and Father said he wished to come too," she added.

He halted halfway to the door and looked over her shoulder at her. "Lord Rockford is joining us?" That put a wrinkle in his plans.

"Yes, we need a decent chaperone, and he will do."

Damnation, how could he be with Alex while her father was watching? A large country mansion like this was one thing, but in a crowded little traveling inn, it would be almost impossible.

He located a footman in the hallway and gave him instructions to reserve rooms at the little roadside inn called the Raven and the Boar, and then he rushed upstairs to see to his own clothes being packed. When he came back downstairs an hour later, he was hoping to find Alex.

"Ah, Worthing, I assume you're returning to London with us?" Rockford stepped out of his study by the stairs, his expression warm, making Ambrose smile, too.

"Yes. Neither Miss Darby nor Lady Alexandra have been there recently, and it will be enjoyable to escort them around the city."

"Indeed! My wife will be shocked I've come, but it will do her some good to see me out and about," Rockford chuckled.

"It will be a pleasure to renew my acquaintance with Lady Rockford."

Lord Rockford nodded. "Agreed." He clapped a hand on Ambrose's shoulder and walked back into the study.

Three hours later, Ambrose stood outside as a four-in-hand carriage was being packed. Alex and her father climbed inside. The lady's maid and a spare footman sat on the boot at the back of the coach. Ambrose gave the driver instructions to collect Perdita Darby before he climbed inside and sat across from Alex.

On the way to Darby House, he and Rockford discussed the joys of shooting and reminisced about past days. He noticed Alex watching him, her eyes soft, her lips curved slightly in the way they did when she was on the verge of smiling without being aware of it. He loved that about her, her constant joy.

When the coach slowed to a stop outside Miss Darby's residence, Ambrose offered to get out and assist Alex's friend inside.

The second he climbed out, his heart stopped. Vaughn stood beside Perdita and her maid, a set of packed valises sitting at his feet.

"What the devil?" he growled, almost falling down the coach steps.

"Worthing." Vaughn inclined his head, a mocking smile on his lips.

"You're not—"

"*I am.*" Vaughn glanced at Miss Darby, smiling. "Here, lad." Vaughn waved a footman over. "Take the lady's luggage." He lifted his own cases and followed the footman around to the back of the coach.

He gave Ambrose a brief moment to speak with Perdita.

"Miss Darby, I thought only you were accompanying us to London." He glanced over his shoulder, watching for Vaughn to reemerge.

Perdita blushed. "Once Mama heard of my plans to go to London, she suggested Lord Darlington accompany me. I'm *terribly* sorry." This last was whispered as she leaned into him a little. It was obvious Alex had warned Perdita about Vaughn's potential danger to her reputation.

"Very well, we shall make do," Ambrose muttered as Vaughn returned. Ambrose assisted Perdita inside, and then he and Vaughn were forced to share the seat opposite the ladies and Lord Rockford.

"Darlington," Rockford greeted. "Glad you could join us."

"Thank you." Vaughn still smiled as he sat down. "Lady Alexandra." He inclined his head toward Alex.

"Lord Darlington," she replied politely, only a hint of caution in her tone.

Ambrose did his best to rein in his surly mood. Now he had to be on constant guard with Vaughn. It was obvious the other man was there to make a go at Alex, but not if Ambrose could help it.

Despite his best intentions to ignore Vaughn, Ambrose spent the late afternoon in conversation with him and the others as they traveled to the inn. It was the earl's fault. He had a way about him that seemed to banish ill will among companions.

It took four hours to reach the Raven and the Boar. Ambrose took care to see to the rooms and was thoroughly displeased to discover he and Vaughn would share a room. Perdita and Alex were sharing. Of course, the earl had his own chamber. It would be another night without access to Alex. At least this would make it easy to watch over Vaughn. Still, Ambrose did not like it when his carefully- laid plans were disrupted. Perhaps he could find a way to get Alex alone, however briefly. If he couldn't steal one more kiss by midnight, he might go mad.

The inn provided simple fare for travelers who didn't wish to pay much, but Ambrose assured the innkeeper that they would need more elaborate fare. He was delighted to see a meal of roast woodcock and pea chick with asparagus along with bread and soup.

The common room was filled with other travelers. The warm, bustling feel of the crowd was something that Ambrose usually enjoyed, but sitting amongst his companions now, he realized he missed the wide-open space of the dining room at Rockford's house in the country. The smell of unwashed bodies and the scent of unclean hay and road-weary horses was not as pleasant as he remembered. There was something to be said for clean stables and rested horses.

After a quiet but pleasant dinner, the ladies left their table to retire to their chamber. Ambrose rose and walked them to the stairs, pausing and leaning in to Alex to whisper, aware of Perdita hovering close by.

"If you want me, I'll wait up. Knock on my door after midnight, and I'll make sure that Vaughn's asleep. We can find somewhere to be together," he whispered.

She bit her lip, her eyes bright, her cheeks pinkened. "See you after midnight."

Their hands brushed, an almost innocent touch, but his skin burned and his body tensed with renewed hunger. He still wanted her, and even after having her once, he *needed* her again. He watched her ascend the stairs to the rooms, the sway of her hips too enticing. His hands itched to grab her hips and pull her back against him. It would feel so good to take her like that, their bodies pressed front to back. He liked to try all sorts of positions, and he'd only been able to try just a few with Alex. He wanted to try everything with her.

"Well, I think I'll retire as well." Rockford yawned, and with a tired smile he bid Vaughn and Ambrose goodnight and went up the stairs past Ambrose, who hadn't moved even when Alex had disappeared out of sight.

It was just him and Vaughn now. *Damnation.* Maybe he would just go up to his room early.

"Worthing, care to share a bottle of brandy with me?" Vaughn had waved over one of the maids who was tending to customers at the bar, and she was handing him a full bottle of what looked like decent brandy. He would have said no, but it could help Vaughn fall asleep if he had some brandy in him.

He pretended to hesitate, his gaze traveling back up the stairs before he finally nodded.

"Very well, one glass."

Vaughn's smile was slight, as though he was surprised

but a little glad that Ambrose had accepted. That treacherous twinge in his heart forced him to admit it might be nice to have a drink with an old friend and forget the years and circumstances that had created a wide chasm between them.

The barmaid smiled coyly as Vaughn slipped her a few extra coins to cover the bottle of brandy and then some. But his old friend didn't even glance at the woman. Ambrose, before he'd met Alex, would have been tempted to give her a kiss and a rakish smile. Now, though, he didn't want to focus on anyone except his sweet country girl.

"Shall we go upstairs? I'm not much for the rest of this company tonight." Vaughn nodded at the happy, boisterous men at the surrounding tables who were singing and laughing.

Ambrose had little interest in being around that crowd either, at least not tonight. All he could think about was Alex.

Vaughn headed up the stairs, and Ambrose trailed behind, hoping he could get his friend thoroughly drunk so he could find a quiet moment with Alex. He and Vaughn entered their room, and Ambrose closed the door behind him. Vaughn collected two glasses from the small tray that had been brought up earlier with some cold meats to tide them over until morning. Ambrose settled in one of two chairs by the healthy fire that was devouring a stack of logs.

Vaughn brought him a glass of brandy, and Ambrose took it, swirling it gently as he leaned slightly toward the fire, his arms resting on his knees.

"Been a long time since we had a drink together," Vaughn mused as he stood by the fire, his palm resting on the edge of the mantle. A small clock sat in the center of the mantle, its silver arms slowly moving to count down the hours until midnight. Ambrose sipped his brandy and counted the seconds, agonizing at how glacially each one seemed to pass.

"It has been a long time." Ambrose glanced his way.

Vaughn stared at the flames, then drank his brandy and turned away from the fire. A melancholy expression filled his eyes, and he caught a hint of longing and regret in those cool depths, softening the other man's eyes.

"Where did it all go wrong?" Vaughn suddenly asked him.

There was no ready answer, no quick thing Ambrose could say. His tongue felt a little heavy with dread at the thought of saying anything.

"I don't know. Gareth was married, and then he lost his wife, and you lost your parents..." *And I lost myself.* The realization was suddenly there, a piece of his life he hadn't wanted to admit had been lost. He wasn't sure what had changed in him in the last few years, but something had. He'd seen Gareth broken and hardened by losing the love of his life. Vaughn had lost his parents and turned to gambling and other means to survive. And Ambrose? He had lost himself in endless seductions, caring less and less for what the poets called love. Because he was afraid—afraid to love. The idea of being with a woman, one he could love and then lose like Gareth had, had terrified the bloody hell out of him.

Vaughn took another sip of his drink, gazing in the flames. "Sometimes I feel as if we're all damned." Neither of them spoke, but there was a strange yet sad camaraderie between them in that moment as they both acknowledged the sorry state of their lives. Echoes of their boyhood laughter seemed to fill his head, and he could remember the feel of the grass beneath his feet as they ran through the meadows.

Once upon a time when we were young and carefree...

Ambrose raised his own glass again and took another drink. He was suddenly bone-weary, a weariness he didn't want to fight. He stood, finished his drink, and gazed at his friend.

"I think I'll just turn in for the night." He took two steps toward his bed, and then the world spun and he blinked, stumbled, and all went dark.

Alex couldn't sleep. She slipped out of bed, leaving Perdita alone, and fetched her dressing gown off the back of one of the chairs by the small fireplace. The silk slid against her skin and whispered against the worn floorboards as she crossed the room to the door. She shouldn't go outside, but if she could get to Ambrose's room...

Honestly, she chided herself, what could they do? There was nowhere they could meet in secret, not while they shared their bedrooms with other people.

She sighed and opened her door just a crack. The corridor was empty. She slipped through the doorway and then stepped into the narrow corridor. It was close to midnight, and the sounds from the main common room below were quiet. She tiptoed to Ambrose's door, her heart beating in her ears as she rapped her knuckles against the wood.

Please let him hear me and wake before Lord Darlington does. He had whispered to her after dinner that he would wait up for her, but neither of them truly thought meeting up would be possible with so many companions traveling with them. But she couldn't deny her desires and her insatiable hunger to be with Ambrose, even if it meant risking so much. She rapped her knuckles a second time and smiled as the door opened. Then when the dim light of the wall sconces lit the face of the person who answered, she froze in shock.

Lord Darlington stood there, completely dressed, his cool blue eyes taking in her state of undress, and then he had the audacity to smile.

"I daresay you were expecting Ambrose, but I will have to disappoint you, darling." He moved fast—too fast. Suddenly she was dragged inside the room and tossed onto the bed nearest the door.

"What are you—" She struggled as Darlington tackled her, a coil of rope in his hands. Alex bit, clawed, and kicked as he forced a cloth into her mouth, silencing her cries. But he was too strong. Several minutes later, her body was exhausted, her every muscle weak, and her breath harsh in the quiet room. Her hands and feet were bound, and a handkerchief had been shoved into her mouth too deep for her to spit out. She lay on her side facing Ambrose, who had slept through the fight in the bed against the wall. He lay fully dressed, on his stomach, out cold. Tears stung her eyes, and she blinked them away. He didn't wake to save her.

Darlington came over to stand in her line of sight. "He can't help you. I drugged his evening brandy. He won't wake until after dawn." He came toward her, and when he moved to lift her into his arms, she flinched. Darlington scowled.

"I'm not going to hurt you. I know you have no reason to trust me, but on my honor I will not." He then lifted her up and threw her over his shoulder. His shoulder rammed into her stomach, making her sick, but she could only make muffled cries for help. He left the room and moved down the stairs into the dark common room of the inn. Alex tried to think. What was he planning to do with her if he didn't wish to hurt her?

The door to the outside opened, and he carried her into the darkness. Then she heard a voice.

"You're packed and ready, my lord," the gruff voice said.

Alex tried to kick out and make Darlington drop her, but he kept a firm hold on her legs and carried her into a coach. She was placed on the seat, and the doors were shut as he joined her, holding tight to her as he tapped on the ceiling of the coach with a cane. The coach jolted forward, and only when they reached decent traveling speed did he let go of her. She slunk far away in the corner, her body tensed, ready to fight should he try to force himself on her. He moved to sit across from her and then leaned forward and removed the gag from her mouth.

"Don't even think of crying out for help. The driver is aware of your situation, and I paid him a handsome sum to keep quiet. No one will hear you since we are far enough away from the inn."

His words sent shivers of dread through her.

"Lord Darlington, why are you doing this?" she asked, amazed that her voice wasn't tremulous. It was as though everything else inside her was shaking.

He sighed and looked out of the coach window, pushing the curtains back to watch the moonlight upon the surrounding fields.

"It is not personal, Lady Alexandra. You've become the subject of a wager, and I dearly need to win."

The wager. Ambrose was right to have been concerned. Maybe Darlington would tell her the details that Ambrose would not.

"What wager?" she asked. "You say it's not personal, but you kidnapped me. I deserve to know the truth."

He glanced her way, a rueful smile upon his lips. "I suppose that is true enough." He let the curtain fall back into place. Only a small shaft of light illuminated his beautiful but cold features. More than ever, she missed Ambrose, his rakish smiles and boyish charm, yet he was just as masculine as Darlington. The difference was warmth. Ambrose was like a roaring fire on a winter's night. Darlington was a cold breeze beneath a beautiful tapestry.

"Someone put your name down in a betting book at White's."

"What are the terms?" She sat up straight, resting her bound wrists in her lap and squaring her shoulders.

"You really wish to know?"

She nodded. "I have to."

He leaned forward then, bracing his arms on his knees. "The man who successfully and publicly ruins you will receive five thousand pounds."

So much? The amount was staggering. A well-heeled gentleman of the *ton* tended to receive ten thousand a year in annual income. She couldn't imagine anyone paying half that simply to ruin her.

"What did the wager require specifically when it said public ruination?" she asked.

"At least three or four gentlemen who could be trusted to speak the truth of what they saw would need to see you in a physically compromising position with a man. Such as being in a man's townhouse in your dressing gown, or even better would be in a man's bed."

Alex swallowed hard at the thought of any man aside from Ambrose seeing her unclothed in a bed. Her stomach gave a violent pitch at the thought of what was to come with Darlington. She tried to regain control and focus on what she needed to know, which was who wanted to do her such a great harm.

"Who would do that?" She racked her mind trying to think of any gentleman who would dare to want to harm her like that.

"His name is Gerald Langley. Do you know him?"

"I've heard it somewhere, but I cannot recall..." The name seemed to dance at the edge of her mind. "And he mentioned me specifically in the wager?"

"Yes, and the requirement was that it be public. It seems he has a great desire to destroy your reputation."

Alex tried to digest this, but a wave of horror and shock hit her as she fully understood how dire her situation was.

"Are you...will you..." She failed to ask if he would force her.

Darlington grimaced. "I'll not touch you, not in that way. All I require is proof that you stayed in my townhouse unchaperoned, and once I've offered that proof, your lover will come to your rescue. I can be most convincing regarding your ruination."

Alex's relief that he didn't plan to force her was momentary.

"My lover?"

He smiled. The expression was smug. "I am all too aware of which man *actually* ruined you. Why else would you show up at our door looking for Worthing after midnight? I'm not a fool, darling. You're besotted with him, and the sad fact is that you have no idea he is a part of all of this." Darlington waved his hand around the coach interior.

"What?" Alex barely got the word out. His declaration had knocked the breath from her body. Surely he was lying. Ambrose couldn't—

"I'm not the man who put his name down in the books beside your wager. Any man could try to satisfy the terms, but Worthing put himself directly into your wager with dozens of witnesses to see him. He's the one who vowed to seduce you in front of a roomful of gentlemen. I'm simply the man trying to beat him to it."

No... Alex's eyes burned with fresh tears, but she couldn't move, couldn't even breathe. Not Ambrose. Not after everything...

Her heart gave a painful beat. Then it seemed to stop altogether as an awful hollowness took its place.

She wasn't sure how long she sat there in the silence of the coach as it rattled toward London. It was likely hours. She was numb by the time they'd entered Grosvenor Square. Pale early-morning light peeped warily through the parted coach curtains of the small windows. Alex gazed at the fine row of houses on Duke Street, watching the predawn light turn the white stones a pale pink and the trees a lovely shade of purple. But she didn't really see it. Her mind was turned inward, dwelling on her pain.

Ambrose had broken her heart, betrayed her, for the sake of some damned wager by a bunch of cruel men in a club. It was all about money, for him and for Lord Darlington. At least the latter had been brave enough to own up to his schemes. Ambrose had truly seduced her, not just her body but her heart. She cringed at how foolish she'd been to let her guard down and let him into her heart.

The coach stopped in front of an elegant townhouse, and she let Lord Darlington escort her up the stairs and inside. There was little point in fighting him off or trying to escape. She was in her nightclothes and dressing gown. If she ran about in the streets dressed like this, it would ruin her and make her appear to be mad. Better to stay with Darlington for now until she could reason out a better alternative.

"This way, my lady." Darlington ushered her to an upstairs bedchamber that, while well furnished, was clearly outdated and a bit unkempt. It was clear Darlington was in dire straits just as Perdita had said.

"Lord Darlington," she began, turning to face him as he stood in the doorway, blocking any escape.

"Yes?" He held his hat in one hand and watched her seriously, his blue eyes cool and calculating.

"What if my father paid you? Would you let me go and not ruin me, at least publicly?" It was worth a shot, however small, to ask him that.

Darlington studied her, and she could see him weighing the options she presented against the wager's payout. There was a flicker of hesitation in his eyes as they softened to pity.

. "That wouldn't work, at least not to save you from

ruination. The bets are a serious thing, my dear. If it wasn't me, another man, possibly one who wouldn't be bothered to leave you truly untouched, would take up the challenge. I don't believe either of us wishes to see you fall prey to another man." He started to leave, but Alex rushed to him and caught his arm.

"Please, Lord Darlington, let me go home. Don't do this." She'd never been one for begging, but in that moment she would've done anything to get free and escape ruination.

"I'm sorry. Truly. It is not to my taste to seduce innocents or even pretend to. But this necessary charade will help me survive a little bit longer before I must sell the clothes off my back." He hesitated and then sighed. "It will be over soon. All I intend to do is bring over the gentleman who arranged the wager and let him see you in my house dressed as you are. That should be public enough, I hope, to satisfy him. Then you may return home. Please stay in this room. There is nowhere else for you to go. I will send up a tray of food shortly so you may break your fast." He bowed and then slipped outside, closing the door behind him and turning the key in the lock.

Alex stood facing the closed door for several long minutes, her heart stinging and her body still numb. What would happen when her father and Perdita awoke to find her gone? What about Ambrose? She banished that thought from her mind. The last thing she needed to worry about was a man who had publicly accepted a wager to seduce her.

If only I had listened to my mind and not my heart that night at the assembly rooms in Lothbrook. We never should've waltzed. He never should've set foot in my home.

She had made too many foolish mistakes, ones that condemned her to ruination and heartbreak. This was worse than when Marshall had left her for a wealthy woman. Far worse. She hadn't given Marshall everything, as she had done with Ambrose. He had her heart, body, and soul. She was the fool who would pay for indulging in such girlish dreams of falling in love and marrying a man who would love her back. Twice she had been burned upon the altar of love, and she was done with it all.

Love be damned.

⚜ 13 ⚜

Ambrose woke to a world where everything was pounding, his head, the door...

"Mr. Worthing! Please, you must wake up!" a feminine voice begged him.

A foggy pain seemed to have settled in his head, and he could barely hear anything aside from the blood pounding in his ears.

He struggled to sit up and realized he was still in his clothes from the night before. Why hadn't he changed? Had Alex come to his room and he'd passed out and missed seeing her? He couldn't remember a damned thing.

"Mr. Worthing!" The voice came again.

He tripped as he tried to get out of the bed. It took him a moment to realize Vaughn's bed was empty. Then he reached the door and opened it, his head still pounding.

"Mr. Worthing?" Perdita was dressed and watching him with shocked wide eyes.

"I...Miss Darby, what's the matter?" He tried to collect his scattered thoughts.

"It's Alex. She's missing. I thought perhaps...she might be with you." Miss Darby glanced around the room, and he couldn't help but wonder how much Perdita knew about him and Alex. "Where is Lord Darlington?" she asked suddenly.

The fog in his head was beginning to clear, and one thought jumped out and clubbed him soundly.

Vaughn and Alex were missing.

"I haven't seen Lord Darlington since last night. Mr. Worthing, you look quite unwell. Are you all right?" Perdita touched his cheek and he flinched. Last night he and Vaughn had been talking, sharing old memories over a bottle of brandy...

"Bloody hell, the bastard drugged me!"

"What?" Perdita gasped. "Why?"

"To get to Alex when I couldn't protect her. Christ, we're in trouble, Perdita." He stumbled out of his room carrying his coat as he rushed to Lord Rockford's room. He pounded on the door until the earl opened it, his brows raised.

"Worthing? What the devil..."

"My lord, we have a situation." He hesitated, feeling Perdita behind him. "It seems Lord Darlington has abducted your daughter."

"What?" The earl's face drained of color.

"My lord." Perdita slipped past him and took the earl's arm. "Why don't you sit down?"

"Good idea," Rockford murmured in a daze as he collapsed into a chair. "Now." He looked up at Ambrose. "Tell me everything you know."

Ambrose took a deep breath and told Alex's father everything about the betting books, except the part where he had agreed to seduce Alex. He was lying to her father about part of this, and it made his stomach roll with nausea. Blood drained from Lord Rockford's face as he listened to Ambrose, and his hands shook so hard he fisted them on his thighs as he sat facing Ambrose. Perdita stood behind the earl, her face a mask, hiding all emotion, which confirmed Ambrose's suspicions that she knew more about him and Alex than he'd first thought.

"So you came to Lothbrook to protect my daughter from those damned rakehells at White's?"

"Yes." It was true, even if he had to omit the part that he was seducing her as part of her protection.

"Lord, what are we to do?" Rockford's face suddenly seemed ancient with grief and worry.

"I will go after them. I believe Vaughn took her back to London. You must escort Miss Darby to London and take the coach. I will ride ahead on horseback. If I find her, I'll bring her to your townhouse, where Lady Rockford should be able to receive us until you arrive."

The earl stared at him, worry and hope colliding in his

eyes, eyes that reminded Ambrose too much of Alex. He dared not think of how frightened she must be. If Vaughn so much as touched her, Ambrose vowed to run him through, their old friendship be damned.

"I suppose that's our only option, isn't it?" Lord Rock-ford said.

"I believe so, my lord."

"Godspeed," the earl said and held out his hand. Ambrose clasped it firmly, making a silent vow that he would find Alex and bring her safely home.

He left Rockford and Perdita to finish packing as he rushed down to the stables to hire out the best-looking horse he could find. It was still a sorry nag that he ended up with, but he had no choice. He kicked his heels into the horse's flanks as he raced down the road that would take him to London. He guessed Vaughn would take Alex to his townhouse on Duke Street, but he must have some idea of how to conduct the public ruination, and that worried Ambrose more.

I'm coming for you, Alex, I swear to you.

TWO HOURS LATER, AMBROSE SLID OFF HIS HORSE AND shoved his reins at a weary groom as he raced up the stairs to Vaughn's townhouse and pounded a balled fist on the door. He'd had a long time to think and to worry, and he'd realized something. He had to save Alex at any cost because he cared about her, cared enough that he was afraid he was falling in love with her. If he couldn't save her reputation from public ruination, he'd never forgive himself, and she'd have to endure society's judgment. And it would be all his fault. He was not going to let that happen to the woman he loved.

A butler opened it a long minute later, yawning as he did so.

"His lordship is not—"

"Stow it!" Ambrose barked and shouldered roughly past the man to get inside the townhouse.

"Sir!" the butler shouted, more awake now that he'd been knocked aside.

"Vaughn? Where the devil are you?" Ambrose bellowed. The old butler tugged at his arm as he started for the stairs, but a door opened to the right and Vaughn came out.

"Ambrose," Vaughn greeted quietly. He was fully dressed, not a hair out of place, but his eyes were weary as though he'd expected this.

"Where is she?" Ambrose charged at his old friend, and before Vaughn could react, he punched Vaughn in the face.

Vaughn staggered back a step and clutched his chin. Blood glistened on his lips as he smiled ruefully at Ambrose.

"Damn, I forgot that vicious right hook of yours." A second later he lunged for Ambrose, his fists raised.

He should have expected Vaughn to fight back, but he wasn't prepared. Vaughn landed a blow to Ambrose's eye that stung, and he clutched his face as he ducked from another swinging fist. Then he bent double and ran at the other man, catching him by the waist and slamming him back against the wall where he pounded his own fist into Vaughn's side.

"Fucking Christ!" Vaughn snarled and threw up a knee into Ambrose's chest. The blow knocked the wind out of Ambrose as he faced his friend, ready to throw as many punches as it took to get to Alex.

"Don't make me ask again. Where is she?" He let his tone go as dark and lethal as his present mood. Ambrose could barely speak. He was raging inside and terrified of what might have happened to Alex.

Vaughn's gaze flickered toward the stairs, betraying Alex's location.

"She's safe and unharmed. I promise that, Ambrose, on my life." He moved slowly but deliberately to block Ambrose's path to the stairs.

"Get out of my way, Vaughn, or I'll hit you hard enough that you will stay down." Ambrose's hands curled into fists.

Vaughn raised a hand. "I understand that, but you have to listen to me for one bloody minute."

Ambrose arched her brow. "Oh? And why is that?"

Vaughn rolled his eyes, something he'd done often

enough when they'd been lads and Ambrose hadn't been able to follow him as quickly on a scheme.

"She is in the betting books. You know what that means. Until the wager is satisfied, she will never be safe, never be free. You know that those other men will never stop. Gerald Langley put a price on her reputation for five thousand pounds. And you and I both know those men won't just stop when it comes to appearances. They'll go for her maidenhead as well."

Ambrose's heart sank as he realized what Vaughn was saying was true.

"Someone has to ruin her to save her," Ambrose said. "It was why I put my name down on the wager. And it should be me. It's why I went to Lothbrook, but I..." He couldn't bring himself to make Alex's ruination public.

"I knew you'd already claimed her, but I also saw how much you cared about her. You wouldn't finish the job," Vaughn said.

"And you needed the coin, didn't you?" Ambrose accused.

"I do." Vaughn paused. "Langley is on his way here. I convinced him to come and see Alex in her nightgown at my townhouse in a bedroom. It will hopefully be enough for him. He can go back to White's and crow over her ruination."

Vaughn's plan, albeit cold in regard to Alex, did make sense. As much as Ambrose was loath to admit it, it was a good idea.

"Then let me be the one he sees. I'll give you the money, but I won't have her tied to your name. It should be mine."

"Because you love her." Vaughn was smiling again, a hint of a wicked gleam in his eyes.

"I do not," Ambrose snapped.

"You do."

Ambrose shook his head. "She's a lovely woman, and her father is an old friend."

"And you and I both know you aren't that good a man. You went out of curiosity, and you fell in love. There's no shame in admitting that." Vaughn crossed his arms over his chest, his eyes serious.

Ambrose struggled for words, but with a heaviness he realized it was true. He was in love with Alex, had been since the night they waltzed. There was no joy, no excitement at the revelation. Rather, his heart had begun to bleed as he faced the truth of the situation.

"She will never love me, not when she knows the truth that I was there to seduce her."

"Yes, unfortunately, that's true. She knows you signed your name in the book."

Ambrose felt like he couldn't breathe. The world was closing in around him, and he was choking to death on the inside. "You told her, didn't you?"

"I did." Vaughn didn't deny it, but he also didn't appear to be gleeful at his admission. "I didn't know you loved her, not until you stormed in here and threw that punch."

"What the bloody hell are we going to do?" Ambrose raked a hand through his hair.

"You are going upstairs to see lovely Lady Alexandra. Come clean about everything and convince her to let Langley see the two of you in bed. Once he is gone, you may take her home. I'll lend you my coach."

Ambrose stared at his old friend. "I'm tempted to hit you again, you know."

Vaughn shrugged, his lips twitching slightly, although still swollen from the first punch. "You can later, but we need to be prepared. Langley will be here soon. She's in the first room at the top of the stairs. The key is in the lock."

Ambrose, who had started for the stairs, froze and then glared at him.

"You locked her inside?"

"She's a strong-willed woman. I didn't want her running out into the street half-clothed. They might fear she's mad. Better to be safe."

Ambrose stalked up the stairs and reached the door. He touched the key and held his breath. Why did it feel like the moment he opened this door, his life would end?

❧ 14 ❧

Alex was sitting in a chair by the unlit fire, staring at nothing. She was aware of shivering, but the sensation seemed so distant, as though her mind and her body had separated ways long ago.

Ambrose had come to Lothbrook to seduce her. She was nothing more than a wager to him, a five-thousand-pound challenge. He'd won far too easily.

First Marshall and now this...

She curled her arms around her chest and lowered her head, closing her eyes as tears leaked down her cheeks. How was she going to survive this? It was as though she'd been ripped away from the safety of her heart's inner fortress and thrown naked on a flat field, unable to protect herself from the world. There was no going back, no way to rebuild those inner walls. It was too late because she'd fallen in love with Ambrose and he'd used her heart against her.

She stiffened her spine and tried to figure out what she was going to do. Any moment now the man who'd started the wager would arrive, and she'd be forced to confront him. What should she do? Fight off Vaughn if he tried to touch her? He'd promised he wouldn't, but what if he changed his mind or Langley demanded he touch her? Yes, she would fight if it came to that. She'd never been a wilting flower, and she was not about to let any man change that about her. Even though her heart was shattered, her pride and righteous fury were making her strong enough to survive. Langley would regret making that bet and so would Darlington for bringing her here.

The sound of a key turning in the lock attracted her focus, and she tensed. Was now the time for Darlington to ruin her? The door opened, her lips parted in shock, and her heart jumped in a treacherous wave of relief. Ambrose stood there, his face pale and his eyes haunted with shadows.

"Ambrose?"

He closed the door and rushed over to her, taking her into his arms and seating himself in the chair with her on his lap. His quick actions surprised her, and she wasn't ready to push him away even though half of her was struggling inside with her rage and hurt. The other half of her was relieved to be safe in his arms. But she knew she wasn't safe, would never be safe again from heartache when it came to this man.

"You are all right, thank God," he murmured, his arms banding tightly around her.

It would be so easy to give in, to let her heart surrender again and seek shelter and comfort in his embrace. If only he'd never agreed to take the wager to ruin her, she could have stayed here in his arms, feeling the warmth of his breath against her cheek and breathing in his scent of leather and sandalwood. Her eyes prickled with tears as reality crashed down around her, and she shoved at his chest. He was too startled to stop her as she climbed off his lap and darted away. She shouldn't have let him touch her or hold her. It was too painful, even so much that it eclipsed her anger at him.

"Alex, I'm here to help."

She put precious distance between them, pulling her dressing gown closed like a shield.

"Please, don't touch me—don't come any closer," she whispered.

He stared at her, his eyes worried, his brow furrowed, and she realized he didn't know why she was angry with him.

"I know about your involvement in the wager." She paused, and the room grew deathly silent, like a tomb that had not been disturbed for centuries. He stared at her as he slowly stood from the chair. Lines of weariness carved paths around his mouth and eyes, which she'd once considered evidence of his love of laughter. When he didn't speak, she continued.

"You came to seduce me for five thousand pounds." The words tasted bitter on her tongue. Ambrose stood but didn't try to come closer.

"It was never about the money, Alex." His voice was deceptively soft, like a man attempting to soothe a spooked horse.

"Oh?" She laughed bitterly.

"No," he growled, a scowl marring his features.

"Five thousand pounds is a lot of money."

"It is, and I never intended to take it."

"Was that because you were more interested in the challenge itself?" She knew her voice sounded shrill, but she couldn't seem to stop herself.

"No. Damnation, woman, let me speak." He moved toward her. "We don't have much time. A man named George Langley is on his way here. He's the man who wishes to see you ruined. We must oblige him."

"Why?" Alex demanded.

He stared at her for a long second, then drew in a slow breath. "Because if we don't, all those other men at White's will come after you, Alex. You will never be safe, not until the wager is deemed satisfied. That has been my goal from the start. To protect you from those other men. Not even marrying you would have saved you. Public ruination is their goal, and that doesn't require you to be unwed. They would not hesitate to rape you, Alex. Do you understand? They are bad men who want that money and will do *anything* to get it."

That thought stopped her cold. She hadn't realized it could be that serious.

"But..." She faltered as she realized Ambrose was right. "What do we have to do to stop them?"

"Langley will need to see you compromised. I'm sorry, my love, but that means you and I in bed..." She saw him swallow thickly, and he continued. "Or you may choose Darlington in bed. Your choice."

Ambrose or Darlington? There was no choice. She hated and loved Ambrose at the same time, and he was the only one she could trust in that moment.

"You. I choose you."

Ambrose's breath blew out in a rush. "Get into bed. I'll listen at the door." He turned away and stripped out of his coat and waistcoat before he kicked off his boots.

Alex settled on the bed, watching him open the door a crack as he listened. They both held their breath for what seemed like forever. Finally, Ambrose tensed, and then she heard masculine voices drifting up the stairs. He closed the door, strode to the bed, and climbed in beside her. She lay back, staring up at him. How different this felt from the other night. That night had been wonderful and inti-mate, and this...this felt like a betrayal of that night.

He cupped her face, his eyes dark and full of concern.

"Whatever happens, trust me one last time, my love, please." He stroked the pad of his thumb over her lips, and her lips trembled. *My love*—the words were a dagger to her heart when he uttered them so casually. How many other women had been his love over the years?

"One last time," she echoed faintly. It felt as though her heart was splintering like fractures in glass, spun as fine as spiderwebs.

He nodded and solemnly lowered his head to kiss her. It felt good and bad all at once. She clenched her hands in the blankets, resisting the urge to touch him. But when his lips parted and his tongue traced the seam of her mouth, she melted. She was lost in the haze of a bittersweet kiss, like tasting the last apple from an orchard in the fall, the sweet fruit carrying a hint of frost as winter crept through the gardens and the trees.

The door to the chamber opened, and Ambrose tensed above her, their lips breaking apart.

Fear gripped her and she closed her eyes, her stomach roiling.

"Hold on to me and don't look away," Ambrose murmured, and she opened her eyes. She could sense a group of men at the door, far more than she'd expected, but as long as she gazed into Ambrose's eyes, she could survive this.

There was a murmur of male chuckles, and then Darlington spoke.

"As you can see she is quite ruined. Shall we discuss payment downstairs?" Darlington's voice was muffled as the door started to close, leaving her and Ambrose alone.

"They are gone," he said, but didn't move off her. "We will wait until Vaughn has seen them out, and then I shall take you home to your mother. Your father knows all that's happened, and he will be waiting at your London townhouse with your mother."

Alex held in the sob that tried to escape. It was over... for now. All of London would know of her ruination in a day, and she would never be able to go anywhere without hearing whispers or enduring sidelong looks.

My life, what little of one I had, is over.

"Are you all right?" Ambrose asked, frowning.

"*No.*" The word escaped her brokenly, and she mustered the last bit of her strength not to burst into tears in front of him. "I'm the farthest thing from it. I need to go home. *Now.*" She shoved his chest, feeling her heart break even further.

He carefully climbed off her and put his coat and waistcoat back on. A minute later Darlington open the door.

"Ambrose, I believe I figured out Langley's motives." Darlington's gaze swept to her, and then she glanced away. She wasn't ashamed. She'd done nothing wrong, at least nothing by choice, but the way she felt in that moment, wounded and vulnerable, she didn't want to meet anyone's eyes.

"Well?" Ambrose demanded as he finished pulling on his boots.

"Langley is the brother to a woman named Hilary Clifford. She married a man named Marshall Clifford a few years ago."

The name Marshall Clifford was a renewed staff to her heart.

"Marshall is involved?" she asked.

Both Ambrose and Darlington turned toward her.

"You know him?" Darlington asked. When she nodded, he continued. "It seems that Marshall has upset his wife by mentioning you too often—old loves fade slowly—and well, she complained to her brother, Gerald Langley. He seemed to think it would please his sister to destroy Lady Alexandra's reputation for being a paragon of virtue and grace."

Stunned, Alex took too long to react as the identity of the man who'd begun the wager sank in. This had been about Marshall and his wife.

"He wanted her ruined because Marshall Clifford was too much of a fool to marry Alex when he had the chance and it upsets his current wife to know that?" Ambrose growled.

"Yes, that about sums it up," Darlington said. "Nasty man, Langley, and Clifford sounds like a fool."

"He is," Ambrose said. "I've met Hilary. She's an ugly woman who believes her position and money entitle her to just about everything. She bought herself a husband but couldn't buy his heart. Foolish creature."

"I should like to go home now." Alex's voice came out barely above a whisper, but both men heard her.

"I'll summon the carriage," Darlington said and met Alex's gaze. "I offer my apologies, Lady Alexandra. I know you have no obligation to forgive me, but I beg for it nonetheless. If there had been another way to save you from the wager, we would have chosen that course of action." Darlington, for once, seemed entirely sincere, which, given his reputation, left Alex feeling strangely conflicted as she watched the impoverished viscount leave them alone.

"Ambrose, I'm ready to leave. Please, let's go," she begged.

"Come on," he said gently and escorted her downstairs and into the waiting coach.

The streets were just beginning to fill with people, and if they did not reach her mother's townhouse soon, she would be spotted in her nightgown with Ambrose. Then again, what did it matter? The damage was done. Her life was destroyed, and her heart lay in crystalline shards at her feet.

❧

AMBROSE'S ARMS HURT WITH A LONGING TO HOLD ALEX. She sat across from him in Vaughn's private coach, her face cold and her eyes downcast. It was as though something had broken inside her—he could see it in the hollow expression on her face and the thinness of her lips. His beautiful, wild Alex was broken.

I broke her.

"Alex..." he began more than once, but she never looked up, and he never continued. The words were trapped inside his head and his heart. They created a pain just behind his eyes and at the back of his throat.

Nothing had ever hurt like this. It was like someone had plunged a dagger into his chest, and with each passing second the invisible blade was twisted deeper.

The coach stopped on Audley Street, and he held up a hand.

"Wait inside the coach. Let me tell them you're here. I don't want you to have to wait outside." He climbed down the coach stairs and then walked up to the townhouse and rapped the lion-headed knocker. It took only a minute for the butler to answer, but Lady and Lord Rockford were right behind him.

"Worthing! Thank God! Is she here? Is she all right?" Rockford demanded.

"Yes, I'll fetch her." He returned to the coach and tried to assist Alex down. She ignored his reaching hands and braced herself against the walls of the coach and then stepped down. She brushed past him without a backward glance and rushed into her mother's arms. Rockford looked between his daughter and Ambrose.

"What happened?"

"We were forced to satisfy the wager—at least in appearance only. She's unharmed, but Gerald Langley, the man who started the wager, will spread the news of her ruination by nightfall." Ambrose held his hat in his hands, awkwardly trying to catch a glimpse of Alex, who was still with her mother in the entryway.

"Come in, Worthing." Rockford waved him in, his gaze somber. "I suppose we ought to discuss the matter of... well...marriage. I assume you are offering yourself after what happened?"

"Absolutely." A day before he would have said no. But now, how could he not? He had helped put her in this situation, his name would always be linked to hers and scandal, and he loved her. Standing there, his hat in his hand, he would beg her to say yes.

"No." Alex spoke up, shocking him and her father. She'd pulled away from her mother's arms and raised her chin proudly.

"What?" Rockford asked.

"I won't marry him, Papa. He came to Lothbrook with the intent to seduce me. He's as guilty of my ruination as Langley and Darlington. I won't marry him. Exile me to the country forever, but I will *not* marry him."

Rockford turned his stunned gaze toward Ambrose, and the earl's disappointment wounded him anew. "Is this true?"

Ambrose swallowed and then nodded heavily. "Yes—"

"Get out. Get out of my house!" Rockford snarled and lunged toward him. Ambrose stumbled back. It was almost as though the older man had struck him. He moved backward until he stood on the steps of the townhouse, and with one last withering look of disappointment and anger, Rockford slammed the door in his face. It smacked into the frame hard enough that the door knocker rattled.

Ambrose didn't move for several minutes. He simply stared at the knocker, his heart pounding and bleeding inside. She didn't want him. Wouldn't have him as her husband. She didn't want him in her life or her heart.

What was he going to do now?

"Sir, would you like me to take you back to his lordship's house?" the driver of the coach asked.

Ambrose nearly said no but thought better of it. He was in a wretched mood, crushed, despondent, and strangely he didn't wish to be anywhere else and certainly not alone.

"Yes, that would be good." There was only one person he could stand to be around right now, and that was Vaughn.

They really were damned.

"Alex, sweetheart, you haven't left the house in days," Lady Rockford said as she entered the small sitting room that faced the street.

Alex was tucked up in the window seat, her slippered feet peeping out from her purple gown. Her cheek rested against the windowpane as she watched the street full of passing carriages and people. Life had gone on outside, just as she known it would, despite her own world crumbling down around her. Talk of her ruination had spread like wildfire the following day. Her mother and father had dealt with the flood of inquiries from friends and acquaintances as well as the withdrawal of invitations from dinners and balls. Their family had become social pariahs in less than a few days.

"Alex, are you listening to me?" Her mother came

deeper into the room and put the back of her hand against Alex's forehead. "You're still too pale, but you feel fine."

Alex gently brushed her mother's hand away. "That's because I *am* fine, Mama."

"Then why not go out with Perdita? You could go riding on Rotten Row or attend the opera." Her mother, still a beauty at age forty-one, couldn't seem to understand why Alex didn't want to go out and enjoy life. But that's because her mother loved parties and people. Alex had always liked quiet evenings at home with a friend, or two at most.

"And endure the looks? The whispers? Mama, you think I am unaware of how much this has cost you? Even Papa has felt the sting of my disgrace. He went to White's today and not one of the men would talk to him. Not one." Alex's eyes blurred with tears and she sniffed, hating the wave of self-pity that overcame her. She'd never liked that particular emotion, but the last week had been unbearable. She'd begged her parents to let her go home, but her mother had said she mustn't run, not from the *ton*. It ought to be faced proudly with one's chin held high. It was much easier said than done.

"Oh, my poor child." Her mother joined her on the window seat and cupped her chin to make Alex look at her. "Now it's time for you to listen. I let you hide when Marshall Clifford broke your heart. That was a mistake. I thought you had too much of your father in you, but I know there is a bit of me in you somewhere. That part of you knows that what those cruel men in the club did was not your fault. You cannot let them shame you. You are *my* daughter too. Do you understand? You will stand tall and proud. Anyone who gives you the cut direct for this is not a friend, and they will not be treated as such."

Alex stared at her mother, and her heart, which seemed to be shredded to pieces in the last week, felt a tiny bit mended. She loved her mother, but until this moment she hadn't really known how much. They were so different and she'd never felt that close before, but now she felt her mother's love burning through her, warming her up.

"Oh, Mama." She hugged her mother.

"There, there, sweetheart," her mother soothed. "Why don't you go riding with Perdita? She's visited every day since you both arrived. I daresay she's quite lonely. I sent a note over an hour ago, hoping you'd go riding. She should be here soon."

"Very well." Alex let go of her mother and went upstairs to change into a riding habit. Her mother might be right. She did feel better at the thought of riding with her friend. By the time she came back down, she found Perdita was waiting for her, looking fine in a blue velvet riding habit.

"Alex." Her friend beamed at her. "The weather is perfect."

And sure enough it was. Alex noted this with wry amusement as she and Perdita rode their horses through

Hyde Park. The weather was sunny and not overly warm, and a gentle breeze stirred the ringlets of her hair against her neck like the fingers of an invisible lover. There were quite a few people on Rotten Row, as gentlemen escorted ladies. The elegant and intricate dance of courtship was being played out in the park. Alex tried not to focus on the happy couples whispering words of love under the watchful eyes of chaperones.

"Alex, how are you?" Perdita asked as they paused to let their horses rest a good distance away from the crowds.

"I—"

"And be honest, please. We've been friends far too long for lies, even well-meaning ones," Perdita said.

Alex stroked her gloved hands along the sleek, muscled neck of her gelding before she spoke.

"Sometimes it's hard to breathe. I think about him and—"

She looked up as she spoke, and to her shock she saw Ambrose and Lord Darlington riding down the path toward her and Perdita. The two men had noticed them and pulled their horses to a stop as if trying to decide whether they should continue or turn back.

"Perdita, let's go," Alex snapped, but it was too late. The gentlemen had made the decision to come their way and were riding hastily in their direction.

Alex went rigid, jerking her horse to a hard stop. There was no way to escape this. Ambrose reached them first, his horse nuzzling hers. The affection between the beasts made the phantom pain inside her surge back to life. She wanted no friendliness, no intimacy, not even between their horses.

"Lady Alexandra," Ambrose greeted, his voice low and respectful. She suspected that he was trying to be soothing, but she was not a mare that needed gentling.

She only answered with a stiff nod. That was all he was entitled to and nothing more.

"Lady Alexandra," Darlington greeted. "Miss Darby."

"Good afternoon, Lord Darlington," Perdita said, then frowned when she saw Ambrose and merely nodded at him.

"Alex," Ambrose said, then ducked his head, shaking it, and tried again. "Lady Alexandra, could I have a moment to—"

"No."

"But—"

She didn't give him another chance. She pulled her horse away, and in a frantic, completely unladylike way, she battled her horse. She bolted her mount away from the group and rode briskly back the way she'd come. She wanted to glance over her shoulder, make sure she wasn't being followed, but she didn't want to give Ambrose the satisfaction of knowing she cared.

"Alex?" An entirely different male voice cut through her panicked thoughts.

She blinked and glanced around. Her heart leapt into her throat. She saw Marshall astride a fine black gelding.

He looked the part of a leisurely gentleman with his well-tailored clothes and his immaculately folded cravat, but he didn't elicit anything in her except sorrow for the innocent young woman she had once been. The fool who thought falling in love was romantic and wonderful.

"Marshall, who is this?" The sharp feminine voice intruded on Alex's memories.

Alex saw a petite woman with a sour face riding sidesaddle on a rather plump brown horse. The woman was glaring at Marshall, and then she turned that glare on Alex.

"Well? Who is she?" the woman demanded.

"She's..." Marshall's face reddened slightly as he struggled for words.

"I'm no one important," Alex replied stiffly, her chin raised as she backed her horse up yet again. What else could go wrong today? She'd run into the last two men in all of England she'd ever wanted to see. At this point, she simply couldn't find it in her to care anymore.

"Wait...Alex? This is Lady Alexandra that you..." The woman was not staring at her curiously anymore, but there was no mistaking the mean glint in the woman's eyes.

Alex snapped. "That he had an understanding with? Yes. He threw me over to marry you for your money. Is that what you wish to hear, Mrs. Clifford?" Her voice was terribly shrill, but she couldn't shake the anger that this woman and Marshall had provoked in her.

Other people riding in Hyde Park nearby were now

watching them, including Ambrose, Darlington, and Perdita.

"Well!" Mrs. Clifford scoffed, her cheeks flushing. It was obvious she had nothing to say to that. So she changed tactics. "It's good then that he threw you over. I hear you're quite the trollop, spending nights in Viscount Darlington's townhouse but in bed with Mr. Worthing, a known rakehell." Hilary smiled cruelly as she announced this loudly enough for the growing crowd to hear.

Alex stared at the other woman for several long seconds, feeling each beat of her heart racing a dozen times between each second. It took her a moment to compose herself.

"Mrs. Clifford, I'm no more trollop than you. As to my ruination at Darlington's house, well, that was orchestrated by none other than a man named Gerald Langley, your brother, I believe. You might ask yourself why he went to such trouble to demean my character and reputation."

"What does she mean by that, Marshall?" Hilary demanded sharply.

Alex didn't wait a second longer to escape. She urged her horse into a quick canter, escaping the gasping, shocked crowd. By the time she reached the townhouse, she was unable to stop the tears. She tossed her reins at the stunned groom who met her by the mews before she raced inside the townhouse and fled to her room.

She flung herself on her bed and buried her face in her

pillow, doing her best to quiet the heaving sobs that escaped. It was a long while later when she finally had cried hard enough that she couldn't shed any more tears and her throat was aching.

She gazed at the window, bleary-eyed and exhausted. She decided upon one thing. She was not going to stay in London. She had faced the worst of it. And now she would go home to the only place she'd ever belonged.

Love be damned.

❦

AMBROSE WORTHING STOOD ON THE FRONT STEPS OF A townhouse on Curzon Street, his hat in his hands as he lifted the knocker and let it drop against the wood. His heart was racing, but that was to be expected. He was about to meet one of the most infamous women in London. The enigmatic Lady Society, the author of the society column in the *Quizzing Glass Gazette*. Lady Society had been penning the most explosive exposés on London society for the last few years. She was ruthless, but she was always true. And he was hoping she could help him—or rather, help Alex.

It had been Vaughan's idea after watching Alex suffer in Hyde Park a week before when she'd faced the sister of the man who'd ruined her over jealousy. She'd fled London and returned home to Lothbrook. The *ton*'s murmurings had been like a hive of bees for the seven days that followed.

Lord Rockford's daughter's name had been on everyone's lips. And it was time they faced the truth. A good, innocent woman had been ruined because of the greed and jealousies of the *ton*. It was a disgrace, and Ambrose was ashamed of being a part of it. But that was going to change, and he was going to give Alex the justice she deserved.

The day after Alex left him brokenhearted and defeated in the park, he began to fall apart, and only Vaughn had gotten him out of his dark tailspin. He suggested Ambrose make an appeal to the one woman society would listen to. So he had to do some investigating, and it had cost him a bit of coin to convince the printer for the *Gazette* to tell him where the columns came from, which led him to a small boy in a bit of a questionable dive. He tracked down two more people, a baker, a modiste, and finally he got to this address. The house on Curzon Street. Of course he hadn't been given a name or a promise—just an address. And even that address he'd only gained after the modiste had him write a letter to be given to Lady Society about his request. The letter from Lady Society came the next day—apparently he'd written the right things—along with instructions to come to this address and bring the letter as proof he was who he said he was.

He wasn't familiar with the man who owned the townhouse on Curzon Street, but he'd known of him. It belonged to a viscount only a few years older than himself. Ambrose was certain that the man was not Lady Society, which begged the question of just whom he would be meeting with.

The door opened, and a young man with reddish hair and brown eyes answered.

"Yes sir, may I help you?" His voice lilted with an Irish accent.

"I wish to speak with the woman who gave me this letter. She advised I give it to the man who answered the door when I arrived."

Ambrose held out the letter and the man accepted it, his eyes running keenly over the words, and then he stared at Ambrose.

"Come inside and wait." He let Ambrose follow him inside, and then he disappeared into a room upstairs. Ambrose studied the fine furnishings of the townhouse, from the gleaming banister to the satin-lined walls and exquisite paintings. There was a portrait of a handsome young man and a dark-haired woman together. The man's laughing eyes and the woman's indulgent smile seemed so intimate that it made Ambrose's chest tighten. He and Alex might never have a portrait like that made with each other. Lord, he wanted that future with her more than anything in the world. He leaned in closer to the portrait, wondering if the woman was Lady Society. If so, she was clearly married.

The man reappeared at the top of the stairs and waved Ambrose to join him.

"The lady will see you now." The man opened the door to the drawing room.

His stomach flipped with a rush of nerves. This woman, whoever she was, could bring the wrath of the *ton* down on him with her pen, or she could save Alex. Ambrose entered a well-lit room with pink damask drapes parted to let the daylight in. A hint of roses filled the air, and he noticed several vases of freshly cut blooms adorning the tables and sideboards. There was no sign of the dark-haired woman from the portrait downstairs; instead, he was startled to find a young woman who couldn't be more than twenty-two seated in a chair. She wore a white muslin gown with flowers embroidered on the hem, and her light-brown hair was pulled up in a loose tumble of curls. She was lovely in a subtle way. In the far corner, another woman sat demurely in a chair, in a pale light-gray gown with no decoration, her hair in a simple chignon as she sewed patiently on a bit of cloth. She was obviously a lady's maid. The young woman did not look up from her needlework.

"Mr. Worthing, please sit down," the lady said and waved to the chair opposite her. A delicate table sat between them, and the red-haired man set a tray of tea upon it.

"Thank you, Sean," the lady said before he left the room, closing the door firmly behind him.

Ambrose took a seat and watched the lady pour tea and offer him a cup. He wasn't in the mood, but he didn't think it would be wise to refuse Lady Society's hospitality. So he accepted his cup and sipped, waiting for what, he wasn't exactly sure.

"I read your letter, of course, and I understand you wish to have my help?"

"Er...yes, for Lady Alexandra."

She smiled. "Indeed. Lady Alexandra has been quite the subject of gossip these last two weeks. As I'm sure you know, I do not repeat tales of that nature in my column. Women have enough to deal with in society these days that we do not need to tear each other apart in smear campaigns," Lady Society said.

"Yes, exactly," Ambrose rushed to agree.

"So tell me, Mr. Worthing, why should I champion Lady Alexandra's cause and fight the stories of her ruination? If talk is to be believed, she has been ruined...in Lord Darlington's house...in bed...with *you*." The lady drew out each of the words, punctuating them delicately as she watched him intently.

Ambrose looked down at his cup of tea, trying to hold himself back from growling in frustration at the entire situation.

"It is true that she was in Darlington's townhouse with me, but that isn't the whole story. My lady..." He paused and then sought the words that would sway her. "Lady Alexandra is the finest woman I have ever met.

What happened to her wasn't justice. It was a plot constructed by a man who wanted to do her harm to please his selfish sister. It is a long tale, but I believe you must hear it. Only then will you be able to judge whether my mission to save her reputation is a noble one."

Lady Society was silent for a long while. The only sound was a little mutter from the lady's maid when she pricked her finger. The soft little disturbance made Lady Society speak.

"Very well, tell me this tale, Mr. Worthing. Leave no detail out."

With a sigh and another sip of his tea, Ambrose began speaking.

"I am no gentleman, but that night at White's when I learned of a man named Gerald Langley's wager to have Lady Alexandra publicly ruined, I had to intervene..."

He left no detail out, not even the details that would've saved his own reputation where Alex was concerned. Lady Society wanted the truth, and if she knew it all, she might become a champion for Alex.

An hour later he was finished with the tale.

"You admit you acted selfishly in pursuing her. And now you are here begging me to expose the truth, even though it will cast aspersions on you?" Lady Society asked.

He nodded. "I've never had the best reputation. It's no loss to ruin it further."

"Indeed, you are quite notorious, Mr. Worthing, but

over the years I've seen worse rakehells than you become the best of men and the best of husbands."

"Husbands?" he queried.

"Yes. I assume that is your desire, that you wish to marry her if we can save Lady Alexandra's reputation. Am I mistaken?" Lady Society raised one brow in challenge. For such a lovely young woman, she certainly had an imperious, commanding presence. He expected nothing less from the woman who penned such brave columns in the *Gazette*.

"I would marry her in a heartbeat, but she won't have me. I am no white knight—I'm just the man who loves her. I ..." The words were trapped in his throat.

"You love her desperately, don't you?" The young woman smiled, her expression sort of soft, almost dreamy.

He swallowed and nodded. "For me, loving her means not eating or drinking and losing sleep over worrying for her and missing the sound of her laugh, the touch of her lips on mine..." He trailed off, hating how foolish he sounded. "I cannot live without her, but if I must, I need to know she's happy, that her reputation and future are secure so that a man worthy of her will find her someday."

The young woman smiled, her eyes glittering with a hint of tears, and she glanced at the young lady's maid in the corner. The maid had stop threading the needle and slowly turned to look at them. Ambrose was startled by the intelligence in the maid's sparkling brown eyes. She glanced between him and her mistress before she set the needlework aside and stood. She spoke to her mistress in a surprisingly familiar tone.

"Thank you, Gillian. I believe it's time we let Mr. Worthing know who the real Lady Society is."

Ambrose blinked and stood in amazement as the maid came over to him and took a cup of tea that the woman called Gillian offered her.

"Here, my lady." Gillian blushed and started to vacate the seat, but the maid gently urged her to sit.

"I am sorry for the ruse, Mr. Worthing, but it is critical to keep my identity secret, you see. This is my maid, Gillian. I am the true Lady Society." The woman dressed as the lady's maid was watching his bafflement with amusement.

"And you are..." He still couldn't guess.

With a secretive little smile she leaned into him and whispered her name and made him swear to never reveal it to anyone upon pain of the death of his reputation if he betrayed her identity.

"I'm sure you know of my brother?" she asked.

He shook his head. "I know of him, have seen him at some of the balls and other engagements in town, but I have not been introduced formally." He was a member of White's, and he knew that Lady Society's brother was a member of Berkley's club. "If you are Lady Society, then you write about him and the League of Rogues, I believe they are called, aren't they?"

Lady Society giggled, the sound pleasant rather than irritating.

"I do indeed. My brother and his friends are in desperate need of matchmaking. I tend to give them a little societal nudge when I see fit."

Ambrose chuckled. "You challenge them, don't you?" He read the articles—everyone had. It was clear Lady Society liked the League of Rogues, but she also teased them mercilessly.

"I do, bless them." She sipped her tea, still smiling. "Now, I've heard your case, and I accept the project. I shall draft a story regarding this wager and have it in the *Gazette* in a few days. I shall also plead your case for you, and God willing, Lady Alexandra will see you for the reformed rake that you are and make a husband out of you."

The relief he felt was only slightly lessened by his fear that what he'd done to Alex was unforgivable. Still, she deserved to have it all exposed, and maybe then she might forgive him. He would love her no matter what, even if he spent the next sixty years watching her and loving her from afar. *As long as she's happy.*

❧ 16 ❧

Alex sat on a stone bench in the middle of the garden in her father's house in Lothbrook, holding a book in her hands. It was a rather boring collection of philosophical essays, but she wasn't really reading it. She was staring at the pages until the letters blurred together, and she was lost in thoughts and memories of Ambrose.

Since she had left London, she had expected to feel less pain, but she hadn't. The wounds in her chest, although invisible, were still there, raw, and as exposed as they had been the morning she'd discovered Ambrose's betrayal.

She blinked back tears and glanced toward the house when her father came out, her mother on his arm. The two had become closer after Alex's ruination. She supposed it was a silver lining to the host of gray clouds thundering above her head.

"Alex..." her father began, his tone hesitant. He glanced at her mother, and she gave him a nod of encouragement.

"Papa?" she queried, a little nervous seeing her father hesitate to do or say anything. It was a rare sight, which meant he had something important on his mind.

"The post arrived from London today. I think you should read the *Quizzing Glass Gazette*, the Lady Society column in particular." He held out the paper to her, and she took it. She didn't miss another look that passed between her parents before they returned inside.

Alex held the paper for a long moment, wondering what could have drawn both of her parents outside to deliver it. It had to be something terrible. She unfolded the paper and flipped page by page until she found the Lady Society column. Her heart stopped, and she began to read.

The *Quizzing Glass Gazette*, the Lady Society column:

Lady Society has much to say today and has a tale of heroes and villains and maidens fair, and even maidens not so fair.

As all of London has been buzzing with the scandal around the ruination of Lady Alexandra Rockford, Lady Society sees fit to put rumors to rest and champion the ruined lady. So, you ask, what truth shall I shed on this matter?

Lady Alexandra was ruined. Yes. That is certain. But it is not her shame, nor by her own choice that such an event came about. No, the villains are the ones to blame. And who are these men?

The gentlemen of White's club who created a wager in a betting book. One identifiable man is George Langley. He initiated the wager out of a desire to please his sister, Mrs. Hilary Clifford, who married Mr. Marshall Clifford, a man who previously had an understanding with Lady Alexandra. So what, pray tell, does Lady Society see in all this? It seems Mrs. Clifford's jealousy of a past woman in her husband's life set her brother on an evil crusade to destroy Lady Alexandra.

Surprisingly, not one man in White's chose to defend Lady Alexandra. Instead, Mr. Ambrose Worthing, a known rakehell, volunteered. He was acquainted with Lord Rockford and knew the depths that the men in the club would go to for a five-thou-sand-pound wager. He believed he could spare the innocent lady pain where these other villains would not. But as fate would have it, the rake fell for the country beauty. If only she could love him back, but no, the ton has shown its cruel side, and we have turned our backs on the innocent woman in all of this. If you wish to do as Lady Society suggests, you will give the cut direct to Gerald Lang-ley, his sister, and anyone who defends them. It is my personal desire to see Lady Alexandra become the most sought-after guest at every social engagement of the season. We who have failed to defend her honor owe her nothing less.

Perhaps, if we are lucky, we might find a way to help mend Mr. Worthing's broken heart, because as I have always said, reformed rakes make the best husbands, and I believe Lady Alexandra deserves the best.

Alex had to read the column two more times before she could admit she even believed what she had read wasn't some elaborate wild dream. Finally, she folded the paper up and walked back into the house, hands trembling. She found her parents in the drawing room. Her mother was seated at one of the small reading tables in the corner, sorting through a massive stack of letters. When she noticed Alex, she smiled.

"Alex, dear, these are for you. They came with the morning copy of the *Gazette*."

"What —" She halted herself and stared at the stack of letters, remembering Lady Society's urging to make Alex a guest at all social events. Surely these all weren't for her...

"You've been invited to every major engagement in London for the rest of the season." Her mother seemed utterly delighted, but none of that mattered to Alex, and her father seemed to notice.

"He hasn't written, Alex," her father said softly.

She glanced his way, knowing what he meant. *He* being Ambrose. Her heart gave a weak thump in her chest.

"*He* hasn't written because he's staying at Darby House. Perdita wrote to your mother two days ago, informing us of his arrival, just in case he attempted to pay a call to you while he's in Lothbrook. I thought you'd be interested to know that..." Her father trailed off, hesitating.

Ambrose was staying at Perdita's? Alex reeled at the thought of him being so close.

"You wouldn't send him away or..." she asked her father

carefully. He glanced down at the book he'd been reading, his cheeks flushed a ruddy color.

"Papa," she said in a tone that she knew he would recognize as a warning.

"Alex, my dear," he said with a sigh. "I was hoping, well, that things might work out. I read the article by Lady Society, and it makes sense. He was a good lad, and he's a fine young man. I was furious about his pretense for coming here, but...if he came, I would not send the lad away. Not if there was some chance that..." He shot a look at her mother, silently pleading with her to help him.

"Alex, what your father is not saying, but someone should, is that sometimes catching a man is not done by conventional means. Take your father, for instance—he might never have married me if I hadn't lured him into the garden the night of our third ball together. He—"

Alex covered her mouth to stop a laugh when her father stumbled to his feet and interrupted his wife.

"Point is, I'm ready to forgive the lad, but the question is, are you?"

Was she?

Alex still held the *Quizzing Glass Gazette* in her hands, and Lady Society's words were tumbling over and over inside her head.

"I don't...I don't know." It was the honest truth. She knew her heart wanted to forgive him, and her body still belonged to him in ways she didn't understand, but her mind wanted answers and time to think before she agreed risk her heart again. Instead, he was there in Lothbrook. So close. She could happen upon him on her daily stroll through the meadows. She could meet him while shopping with her mother in the village. She couldn't go anywhere without the possibility that he could also be there, and she wasn't sure if she could live her life that way. What would she say to him? What did she even want to say? They had parted ways when her ruination had been imminent, and she'd vowed never to marry him. There was a huge part of her that was still furious with him for what he'd done. But after reading Lady Society's article, she realized that the situation had been as dire as Darlington and Ambrose had tried to tell her it was. Men in the clubs wouldn't have stopped coming after her, even if she had been married. Married ladies could still suffer public ruination, after all.

He had said he'd wished to marry her, but had that been an offer derived from pity for her situation or guilt at having caused it? She didn't want a man to marry her for either of those reasons. She wanted a man to marry her because he couldn't live one more minute of his life without her. Was it so wrong to want a man who loved her desperately? If she assumed Ambrose did in fact love her and had wanted to marry her for that reason, she had stoutly refused him. A sensible man would have honored her wishes at the time, and he might have hardened his heart to her. The thought made her stomach churn, and she pressed a palm to her abdomen.

What if he had moved on? Surely he had his pick of

women and wouldn't wait around for her to decide if she could trust her broken heart in his hands for a second time. He was a rake, after all, and they had plenty of women they could turn to, as charming men always did. But her heart insisted that he wouldn't, that what had transpired between them had been different for him than with any other woman.

Is it my vanity that believes such nonsense? Or is my heart so foolish that it has convinced me I was special to him, just as he was to me?

"No one is requiring you to marry him," her father said. "But I thought you'd want to know he was nearby. A man who isn't madly in love would not be waiting at Darby House for you. Trust me." Her father chuckled. "Mrs. Darby is not what single young men frequently choose for company, not when she has been husband-hunting for her own daughter. Why don't you take a walk, think on it? You know how I feel about fresh air for one's constitution." He puffed up proudly, which made her mother giggle.

"Walk? She doesn't need to walk. What she needs is to march up to Darby House and catch that young man in a parson's mousetrap, is what. We can't let him run back to London, not when Alex could be married before the year is out."

"Dear," her father intoned gently, with a great patience he had perfected over nearly two decades of being married to his wife, "she's not going to rush this. It's her heart, her life. Marriage is a serious business, and she ought to make sure she's ready to forgive Worthing and give him a second chance." He turned back to her. "Take a walk," he encouraged.

She sensed he was saying more with his words than that. His eyes were serious, and she could almost hear him saying, *Stop hiding. Face him and you'll know where you stand.* It was why she loved her father. Because he knew just what to say, even just with his eyes when words weren't needed.

"Perhaps I will take a walk," she said.

Her mother made a soft little disgruntled noise and muttered something that sounded suspiciously like, "As long as the walk takes you to Darby House..."

Alex nibbled her lips and then, still carrying the *Gazette* with her, went up to her room to change. It would do her some good to walk and clear her head. Then she might write Perdita and invite her to tea to discuss a strategy about Ambrose. And well...perhaps there was still a chance for her and Ambrose.

჻

AMBROSE HADN'T MOVED FROM HIS SPOT ALONG THE small country road that led to Alex's house in two hours. It had become his daily ritual since he arrived at Perdita's house two days ago. He'd promptly and anxiously answered Perdita's invitation, an invitation made in

London after reading the *Quizzing Glass Gazette* and deciding, she'd told him, that she would give him a chance to prove his worthiness, if he so desired it.

The last two days he had left the house early in the morning to come here and wait with Perdita's words in his ears: *Prove to her that you are worthy of her.*

He hoped she would come out onto the road and he could run into her. He was too afraid to go up to the door and face her father's wrath and Alex's coldness if she didn't want him. He had this odd feeling that if he could see her alone, he might stand a better chance of winning her back.

He would *never* be worthy of Alex, but he wanted to try to be, every day for the rest of their lives. He straightened against the stone wall that lined the road when he saw a woman emerge from a garden gate leading to the Rockford estate. His heart leapt, and he sucked in a breath as he stared hard at the distant figure, and then he couldn't stop the eager smile that split his face.

It was Alex. He would recognize her lovely figure anywhere.

"Come this way," he muttered, praying.

For once, Lady Fate took pity on him. Alex walked in his direction, her head down until she was but twenty feet away. She seemed lost in her own thoughts, something he quite adored about her.

When she looked up and saw him, she froze. Her cheeks pinkened and she stood still, like a startled doe in the woods. His heart beat against his ribs, and his hands

LAUREN SMITH

trembled, so he clenched them into fists. A dozen thoughts raced wildly through his head, but then he realized there was nothing he could say right away that his heart and body could not say better.

He strode up to Alex, and before she could speak or protest, he cupped her face and leaned down, slanting his mouth over hers in an explosive kiss. He wanted her to feel his heartache, his love, his desire, and every complex emotion that had been tearing him up inside for the last fortnight since they'd last seen each other. She melted at first, giving him everything he'd been starving for, but just when the kiss seemed on the verge of being out of control, she pushed his chest. It took every bit of him that was still gentlemanly to let her back away, because the last thing he wanted was distance between them.

Alex's lips trembled as she gazed up at him, and it made him want to drag her back into his arms and hold her forever. He would fight the entire world to make her smile again.

"Ambrose..." She bit her lip, then continued. "I read the Lady Society column." Her eyes were shadowed now, and a terrible fear surged inside him. His and Audrey Sheridan's grand plan hadn't worked. She didn't want him. She didn't trust him, she wasn't going to—

"I'm terrified," she blurted out.

It took him a few seconds to process her words, and he nodded, smiling sheepishly. "So am I."

"You are?" she asked, delicate brows swinging up in surprise.

"Yes." He was still cupping her face, and the feel of her smooth skin beneath his palms was soothing.

"What are you scared of?" she asked.

Ambrose closed his eyes and blew out a deep breath before he continued. He had to make sure she understood just how much she mattered to him and how much he adored her. If he didn't get it right, he could lose her all over again.

"I'm afraid that I'll have to live every day of the rest of my life without you. For a man in love, it's the most terrifying destiny he can imagine." There, he'd said it, the words that would either save him or condemn him.

"You—you mean that?" Alex brushed back a lock of her hair that the wind had been playing with.

"Every word. Alex, I've never loved any woman before. You came into my life like a shooting star. That night we met at the ball, it changed me. I wasn't whole, not until I met you. That damned wager turned out to be the best thing that could ever have happened to me. I hope you don't despise me for saying that."

She tilted her chin to one side, and he sensed she was thinking deeply over what he'd said.

"You are right. That wager was the worst thing to happen to me, but it was the best thing, too." As she said this, he glimpsed that vulnerability she often sought to hide from him and the rest of the world. He didn't want her to hide, not from him.

"I am yours if you want me," he said. "I would give you everything to make you happy," he vowed. And he almost smiled as he realized Lady Society was right. Perhaps reformed rakes did make the best husbands.

Alex's eyes were full of tears, and she nodded. "I do want you. And you really want me too? I thought you didn't want to be tied to one woman for the rest of your life?"

Cursing softly, he dragged her into his arms and kissed the crown of her hair and held her tightly. "I was so bloody wrong. You're the only woman I want in my life."

Finally, he let her go and eased down onto one knee, holding her hands in his.

"Alex, my love—"

"Yes." She cut him off, laughing.

The blossom of joy in his chest was so overwhelming that he couldn't speak right away. He simply stared up at her, speechless, breathless.

"Ambrose, are you all right?" she asked.

"I thought I'd have to convince you," he explained, swallowing the lump in his throat.

"You did...by having Lady Society tell the truth. You fought the entire *ton* for me. If that isn't a test of your love, I don't know what else could be." She rubbed at the tears that were glimmering in her eyes.

"Finding Lady Society was quite the challenge, but it

was worth it to win you back," he admitted. "And it has been exceedingly rewarding to watch Gerald Langley, his sister, and Marshall Clifford become complete social pariahs. No one will invite them to anything now. It's been thoroughly satisfying. Although Langley has vowed to discover who Lady Society is and make her pay for it. I've made a promise to keep an eye on him in the club in case he makes any wild bets that put the dear lady in danger."

"Danger?" Alex gasped.

"Oh yes, Langley is furious. But the lady has been warned, and Vaughn and I are watching out for her. I owe her everything."

Alex relaxed and smiled at him as she pulled him to his feet. "She certainly deserves two knights in shining armor to protect her. I'm glad she has you and Vaughn keeping watch. Who is she, really?"

Ambrose grinned down at her. "That is one secret I swore to take to my grave."

"What? You can't tell me?" She giggled as they began to walk arm in arm toward her home. Lord, he had missed the sound of her laugh.

"I cannot, but perhaps," he teased, "if you start guessing now, you might discover her true identity in the next ten years since there are quite a few ladies to guess from."

"Oh! I can't believe you won't tell me!" she gasped in mock outrage and lightly nudged him with her elbow. "Let me see..."

Alex began to name ladies back in London, and he shook his head, denying each of her guesses. And in that moment, Ambrose realized he had finally found himself. Right here in this moment, walking down a country road with Alex at his side, his heart was fit to burst with joy. Who knew that accepting a wicked wager in a betting book would lead to the love of his life?

When they reached the garden gate entrance, Ambrose pulled Alex in for another kiss. She feathered her lips against his before she opened her mouth to let him delve deeper between her lips. She was bold, his sweet country lass. He loved the way his knees shook and his heart raced as he held *his* woman in his arms. From now on he would always bet on love in any wager.

Thank you for reading *The Rakehell's Seduction*. If you want to know what happens to Vaughn and Perdita, turn the page to read 3 chapters from *The Rogue's Seduction*!

THE ROGUE'S SEDUCTION
CHAPTER 1

L ondon, *December 1821*

Perdita Darby tugged the hood of her cloak close about her face, shielding herself not just from the bitter wind that battered the hackney coach she'd hired, but from any watchful eyes lurking in the shadows. The street was empty, twilight and the cold having chased even the most dedicated late-night strollers to their homes. Even the street urchins, usually desperate for coin, were tucked away in their alleyways on a bitingly cold night such as this, seeking what warmth they could. Perdita feared the darkness might hide someone who would realize who she was or what she was going to do. That could spell ruin.

"M'lady?" The driver of the hired coach stood by the door and closed it as she tugged her skirts free. He began to doff his cap at her, but she waved for him to keep it on.

The night was too cold for such things. He smiled gratefully and kicked the snow off his boots.

"Please wait for me here." She pressed a few coins in his palm, and he nodded.

"Of course." The driver pocketed the coins and climbed back up onto his seat. He bundled his heavy brown cloak over his body and huddled down for warmth.

Perdita faced the door of the townhouse in front of her. It was a lovely home, one that had been on Duke Street for many years. The noble arches were framed with ivy that grew up from the flower beds bordering the windows, even though the leaves had dropped away to expose the skeletal webbing of vines beneath. But in spring when the ivy was bright and sprawling, it would make this house look almost like a cottage deep in the Cotswolds, not a stately townhouse in the midst of a bustling city.

It was clear the owner of this house didn't bother with a gardener who would have kept the ivy from spreading. But that shouldn't have surprised her. She knew the owner of this house. Perdita planned to throw herself at his feet and beg for his help if she had to, and it didn't matter if ballroom whispers called him the Devil of London.

She squared her shoulders.

Be brave. He's the only one who can help you. Don't let him know how frightened you are.

She marched up the steps and rapped the metal knocker mounted on the stout oak door. Suddenly doubt assailed her. This was a terrible idea. Her mind screamed at her to flee as she stood upon the threshold to the underworld.

Perhaps she could beg her parents to let her go to the continent for a few years and avoid the fate that had driven her to this door at such an hour. Yet that would only spare her, not her family, of the consequences of running away from the blackmail she was facing.

The door creaked, the old oak protesting as the hinges grudgingly gave in. A middle-aged butler stood there, his beady eyes peering down at her over his long, thin nose and pointed chin. His professional demeanor lacked the politeness expected of a servant in a decent household. His shoulders were broad, and he seemed far too muscular for a refined position of a butler. But this wasn't a decent household. This was the devil's own home.

"Er..." He blinked at her, apparently startled by her appearance. It was a risk to be seen standing on this particular doorstep after midnight, a fact of which she was all too aware.

"I must see Lord Darlington at once," she told the man, praying he would let her inside. She could not take the risk of being seen and starting a scandal. Or rather, a different scandal than the one she was meticulously planning already.

The man hesitated, his body barring her entrance through the still partially closed door. "This is late, even for my master."

Perdita didn't back down. "I am aware of the hour, but he will want to see me." She raised her chin and announced this with such regal bearing that he would not dare question her. He sighed and stepped away from the doorway. Her mother's lessons, it seemed, hadn't been wasted on her after all.

"This way, madam." He waved a hand for her to step inside. She entered the townhouse, her body relaxing, but only just. She may have been out of view of the street, but she was still in very dangerous territory.

Two dim lamps illuminated the hall and staircase. She was surprised they were still lit. Was the master of the house still awake? She had assumed he would be, but the house was hushed and ghostly quiet. She took a moment to study her surroundings with open curiosity. The foyer was bare of any decorations, paintings, or even end tables. The starkness of it surprised her.

So this is where the Devil of London resides.

The furniture she glimpsed through a cracked-open door a few feet away—the drawing room perhaps—was outdated and threadbare. It made sense. The master of this house was rumored to be a desperate fortune hunter in dire straits. His desperation was no fault of his own, but rather due to his parents' untimely deaths and their accumulated debts.

It had to be a heavy burden to enter adulthood with the responsibilities of maintaining title and lands held in one's own family without any money by which to do so.

Any man in such a position was a *dangerous* man—particularly when it came to rich, unmarried heiresses.

Like me...

"Please wait while I speak to the master. Who shall I say is calling?" the butler asked.

"Perdita Darby," she said, trying to still her trembling as she watched the butler go upstairs.

Perdita swallowed the knot of fear in her throat. This man had been desperate enough to kidnap her dearest friend, Alexandra Rockford, in order to win a five-thousand-pound wager by seducing her. That alone earned him his nickname in her eyes. To treat a woman's virtue as something to be wagered on! In the end, however, he had failed. Alexandra had been rescued by Ambrose Worthing, a man so in love with her he had fought his best friend to free her.

Alexandra had assured Perdita that Lord Darlington hadn't been *entirely* wicked—he'd only planned to convince the men involved in the wager that he had bedded her when he had not. But that did not make the Devil of London a hero, by any means. At best, he was a villain with a conscience. But Perdita was desperate enough to risk herself in his house tonight, knowing the danger and scandal that could fall upon her.

This is a terrible idea. Unfortunately, she had no other option. Only Lord Darlington could help her. She was prepared to do just about anything to escape her situation.

"Madam." The butler appeared at the top of the stairs. "His Lordship will see you now."

Perdita stared up at him, startled. "Upstairs? Not the drawing room?"

The old codger had the audacity to grin at her. "He insisted you meet upstairs, or I was to show you out."

The nerve of the man, demanding she meet him upstairs! Did he treat all gentle-bred ladies like this? Or, knowing who was paying a call upon him, he was perhaps doing his best to frighten her off. Yes, that must be it. He thought she would be too afraid to go upstairs.

I'm not afraid. Well, I am, but I'll be damned if I let him know that.

She lifted her skirts and ascended the stairs, her heart hammering. She followed the butler to a room where the door was slightly ajar. She glanced at the servant, but he was already departing.

Perdita pushed the door open and froze when she realized it was a bedchamber. Darlington had the audacity to call her to his *bedchamber*? Did he believe she had come for amorous reasons, or that she would condone such a brazen attempt at seduction? It was entirely possible, given the scandalous hour and the fact she was without a chaperone, but she would set him straight if he dared to try to seduce her.

She wished for the hundredth time it would have been possible to visit him during the day, but there had been no alternative. People would have seen her enter his home, and that would be the end of her carefully kept reputation. She tensed when a dark, rich voice spoke.

Vaughn Darlington, the viscount dubbed by *ton* as the Devil of London. His voice sent tingles of excitement and fear through her. She took an instinctive step back toward the door.

"Fleeing so soon? I would have wagered you were braver than that, Miss Darby. Or perhaps, given the lateness of the hour and the method of this meeting, I should call you Perdita?"

She bristled and pushed the hood of her cloak back to better peer around the room. There was a four-poster bed against one wall and a fire crackling in the hearth. The wood floor showed dusty outlines of where carpets had recently been. The dark-green brocaded curtains about the bed were faded, and a few rings were missing, letting the fabric gape in odd places. Worn and peeling silk wallpapers depicting men hunting in the forest covered the walls. A once beautiful wardrobe stood in one corner, a door missing. The shaving stand held a white china basin with a large crack down its side.

The masculine air of the room was overpowering, just as the man himself was, but the circumstances and the condition of his rooms filled her with a strange pity that made her go still as she turned her focus on the man himself.

Leaning against one worn, ancient chair was Lord Darlington. He was tall, broad shouldered, and had a dangerous look about his all too beautiful face. With piercing blue eyes and light-blond hair, Darlington could have passed for an angel if it weren't for the sensual, wicked curve of his lips. He wore buff trousers and a white lawn shirt, with a dark-blue waistcoat. His cravat had been untied and lay loose over the back of one chair.

Perdita's heart quickened. She had never stood in a

room with a man in a state of partial undress like this. She forced herself to rally to the task at hand.

"Lord Darlington, I come here with a proposal." Her tone was brusque with a manner of business about it. This was not about seduction, no matter how sinful he made her feel. Though she'd rehearsed this speech a dozen times on her own, she had not been prepared for the strange and frightening feelings that assaulted her now as she spoke to him alone.

He crossed his arms as he studied her with that wicked twist of his lips, making her breath quicken. She shifted in place, and her boots scraped softly against the wood floor.

"Do go on." He chuckled, seeming to enjoy her discomfort.

"Well, you see…" She spoke haltingly, still mortified that she was here begging him for his help. "I need to stop an unwanted marriage proposal." She twined her fingers nervously as she removed her gloves. "My mother has convinced a certain gentleman that I am willing to consider his offer, when I most certainly am not."

She tried not to think of Mr. Samuel Milburn and how that man had made it clear he would imprison her in a life that would slowly kill her. She could still see him leaning in close to her and whispering: *"The women I care for know better than to seek the company of others, when I should be enough. My home has all you will need, so I will hear no talk of travel or nights out. They would only distract you from your duty, which would be pleasing me."*

He was a brute and a tyrant and worse, but Perdita's mother, despite her ambitious nature, didn't usually believe in society gossip.

Perdita did. She'd heard that Milburn had thrown a woman to her death from a window, but because the woman was his mistress, no questions were asked. It had been dismissed as an unfortunate accident. All Perdita knew for sure was that this man was a monster. She had tried to tell her father and mother what she'd heard, but her words had been dismissed as idle talk. If her older brother Thomas hadn't been away at sea serving in His Majesty's royal navy, she would have sought his help.

In Perdita's experience, being a wealthy heiress was a terrible burden. It put a mark on her. She'd fought off fortune hunters for the last few years, but a man like Milburn was dangerous in other ways. He didn't care about her money—he cared about breaking her spirit and possibly even killing her if she didn't give him what he desired. She was *sport*.

She'd made the mistake of meeting him at a dinner party last fall, and he had immediately shown an interest in her once he'd learned she was none other than Miss Darby, the beloved lady of the *ton* who all sought to please with their praise and their many invitations.

Perdita had not wished to cultivate such a favored reputation on purpose, but it had happened quite naturally. But to Milburn she became a prize he wished to win —and then suffocate and destroy. Once he had her in his sights, he had been able to contrive a scheme that could destroy her family and blackmail her into accepting his proposal.

"What does this have to do with me? Or did you merely wish to tumble in my sheets to avoid marrying some silly young buck? I don't care much for ruining innocents, but in your case I might make an exception," Darlington said, his sharp gaze on her.

Perdita considered reminding him he had in fact attempted to ruin her innocent friend over a wager, but she thought better of it. Quarreling with him now would not aid her in acquiring his help.

"I wish to engage your services." She still couldn't say the words. It was too humiliating.

"My services?" He shifted slightly, a frown curving his lips. "What *services* do you require?" When Darlington said *services*, it sounded sinful, wicked.

"I wish to hire your cooperation in appearing to be engaged to me, publicly. Not a true engagement, just for a few months, to deter the other gentleman so he will leave me be." She glanced down, playing with her gloves. She was betting that Milburn would lose interest if he believed he had another challenger for her hand.

His eyes turned wintry, almost chilling as they settled on her fidgeting hands. "So I'm to play your fiancé? What's to be my reward in scaring the bounder off?" Darlington still leaned against the side of the chair, but Perdita was more aware of him than ever. The small distance between them seemed to shrink every second.

"I will pay you. I have access to some of my dowry. It is invested in a private bank with Lady Rosalind Lennox. My father put the funds in his name, but he allows me to have some control over them."

Darlington stroked his chin. "I require a more permanent solution than a temporary flow of money. You said you bank with Lady Lennox?" He continued to stare at her with that assessing gaze, and she suddenly feared he might not agree, that he might consider blackmailing her directly for her funds in the bank by exposing her visit to his townhouse. Surely he wouldn't dare.

When he still gazed at her expectantly, she realized he awaited some response to his question. She nodded.

"Then you are acquainted with Lord Lennox, her husband? He is a selective but successful investor. I wish to be involved in whatever scheme he chooses to invest in next."

Perdita nodded again. She was well acquainted with Rosalind Lennox, but she only knew of her husband, Ashton Lennox, in passing. Perhaps she could persuade Rosalind to allow Darlington to invest with her husband. She only hoped such a request wouldn't seem inappropriate to her friend. It was a risk she had to take to avoid marriage to a man like Samuel Milburn.

"I believe I can arrange a meeting. As to whether he

allows you to invest..." There was no way she could guarantee that.

Darlington pushed away from the chair and came up to her. The simple action seemed to change everything between them. Before he hadn't seemed so threatening. But now with his towering frame so close, she felt very much like a tiny rabbit facing a very large wolf. She knew he was tall, but standing inches away from him made her feel small and feminine in a way she never had before. It took a moment for her to catch her breath. She had to tilt her face back to look up at him.

"I suppose that would be good enough. But you know once we have begun this charade, everyone will expect us to marry." It sounded like he was warning her. They would never marry. If there was one thing she was certain of, she would *not* marry the Devil of London.

"I am aware of that. After a time I deem prudent, you may cry off our engagement and go on as you please." She had to be completely sure Samuel Milburn was no longer interested in her, and only then could she risk a public break with Lord Darlington. Otherwise, her family's reputation would be ruined, and her father might be facing penalties under English law.

His lips twitched in an amused smile. "And you are ready to brave the *ton* after being jilted by me?" The wolfish smile that stole across his lips was not reassuring. "I doubt any other man would have you once I've been your lover."

"We would not be lovers, only engaged."

Darlington laughed softly. "Any woman I asked to marry me would certainly be my lover beforehand. I wouldn't wish to marry a woman unless I was positive I enjoyed my time with her in bed."

She ignored his scandalous words. "Being jilted by the likes of you, even if some assume we've been lovers, is better than having a man like Samuel Milburn find a way to compromise me. I know the sort of man he is, and as unbelievable as it is, he is *worse* than you." She threw her shoulders back and glared at him, daring him to argue the point.

"Milburn?" Darlington's eyes widened. "That's the man who is chasing your skirts?"

"Yes. Do you know him?"

He nodded slowly. "Unfortunately, I do. We've run into each other at various clubs." He paused as though choosing his words carefully, weighing what she ought to hear or not as the case might be. "Most of the *ton* see him as a delightful gentleman who could do no wrong. Others know him as I do. Some would say he and I have similar tastes in pain—not in receiving it but causing it."

"A taste for pain?" Perdita shuddered. She'd heard Milburn had thrown his mistress out of a window. Any future with a man like that would seal her fate, but she hadn't heard the same of Darlington. He wasn't cruel, though she'd heard he was impossibly *wicked*. Even a fleeting kiss upon the hand during an introduction had been known to cause such scandals that ladies in the ballroom took flight to escape, like a flock of birds dressed in silk and tulle.

"Yes." Darlington's eyes were on her face again. "We require something a little different in our bed play." He paused again, his eyes dark and fathomless as he stared at her. "But unlike him, my goal is *always* pleasure. A crying, hurting woman is not arousing to me. But for Milburn, it makes his blood turn to fire."

Darlington's bold words on such a subject made her take another step back.

"You like to cause *pain* in bed?" She hated how her words trembled as they escaped her. Surely whispers of this would have reached her if that were true. "This was a mistake. I should—"

He reached up and cupped her cheek when she tried to pull away, then wound a strong arm around her waist, her cloak bunching above her bottom. She had to face him now and hear whatever it was he wished to say.

"There are two types of pain, love. One is slight, expected, and leads to intense pleasure. The other is selfish and part of a need to be cruel and harsh. I prefer the former, not the latter."

His words didn't make any sense. Pain was pain, wasn't it? She wrinkled her nose and prepared to argue this, but she never had the chance. He lowered his head and captured her mouth with his. Perdita was frozen in shock. The feel of his soft warm lips moving over hers was strange but increasingly delightful.

She'd never been kissed before but had often imagined how it would feel. She mimicked his mouth and gasped as he licked the seam of her lips with his tongue. The velvety feel of his tongue touching her lips was both sinful and decadent. Her knees went weak beneath her heavy skirts. She grasped his shoulders, frantic not to lose hold of him. The heat between their mouths intensified, and a heady dazed feeling began to slink through her limbs and into her lower belly. She could do this for hours...

His lips wandered from hers down to her throat just above where her cloak covered her shoulders. He placed a kiss there and then suddenly nipped her skin with his teeth. The bite sent a jolt through her, and a fierce, shocking pulse beat between her thighs. She whimpered and tried to push away, not because it hurt, but because the rush of sensations had been too much. She'd never—

"That, my love, is pain mixed with pleasure." Darlington whispered this against the skin of her throat, still holding her fast so she could not escape. Shivers rippled down her spine, and she closed her eyes. This was frightening. *He* was frightening, but a part of her wanted to understand more of what he was showing her.

From the moment she'd first seen him at her mother's garden party a few months before, she'd been intrigued by his mysteries. She wouldn't deny it. Any decent young lady would not have allowed herself to be fascinated by such a

notorious rogue, but now more than ever she wondered if
perhaps she wasn't as decent as she ought to be.

Darlington slowly released her waist, but the hand that
still held her face seemed to burn her skin. He brushed his
thumb over her lips, leaving a tingling sensation that
trailed from her mouth down to her toes. She raised her
eyes to his, her world tilting on its axis as she stared up at
him. There was no going back from that kiss. She'd taken
a bite of the forbidden apple, and the juices were sweet
upon her lips.

"You're still trembling," he observed, his voice was low
and gentle, but rather than soothe her, she felt excited
by it.

"It is always like that?" she asked, wondering why
Mother had never mentioned that lips could meet in such
a blaze of fire when she'd discussed the ways men and
women could be together.

Darlington touched her lips once more before dropping his hands. "Not always. Too many marriages are built
upon the wrong foundations, and passions are rarely taken
into account." He turned away from her and walked over
to the fire, placing one hand on the mantle as he gazed
into the flames.

"If you want to play this game, Miss Darby, it must be
played convincingly. Milburn won't accept a mere declaration of our engagement. He knows me too well. He's also
not the sort to give up easily." Darlington's face was lit by
firelight. For a moment, he looked more like Hades, the

Greek god of the underworld, than a mere London rogue. Perdita was entranced by the sight of him. He was a lure she couldn't resist. How many women had come into his room before her and fallen under his spell?

"What did you have in mind?"

"I suppose you recall what befell Alexandra Rockford in my home? A public display. *That* is what I mean. Milburn will need to see us in a compromising position." He turned to face her. "And that means more than a simple kiss."

Perdita bit her bottom lip. A simple kiss? Not to her. That kiss had been her undoing. She was wise enough to know he had changed her life in a few short minutes.

"If it helps me escape Samuel Milburn, then I agree to do whatever is necessary." She raised her chin, earning a slow smile from him that made her blush.

"What?" she demanded as he continued to smile at her.

"I never would've guessed you would agree. Of all ladies, you seem to be the most..."

Perdita narrowed her eyes. "Most what?"

"Let us say I'm surprised at your defiant streak, that is all."

Perdita stared at him challengingly. "I behave appropriately in public, a dutiful daughter and a well-bred lady, but you have no idea what sort of woman I really am." He truly didn't. She was a lady, well-versed in conversation, a charming hostess, a delight among the *ton*, but that wasn't all she was. There were other, hidden sides of herself she dared not reveal.

Darlington's eyes sparkled with mischief. "Now *that* is most interesting. As your fiancé, I will make it my sacred duty to uncover these hidden facets of your character."

She tilted her head, studying him in return. "How about your services then?" She wanted to keep this matter as businesslike between them as she could manage. He would no doubt rob her of her good sense with his kisses, but if she held fast and reminded them both this was only business and nothing more, then perhaps she might survive this devil's bargain with her heart intact.

"I have one last question before I agree, and I demand honesty in your answer."

She weighed the risk of losing his help against any question he might demand and then nodded. "Ask."

"What hold does Milburn have over you that leaves you in such fear? I do not believe for a moment that your parents would force you to accept a match with him even if he dragged you down with scandal. No, there is something that makes you fear you might have no choice to accept if he pursues you." Darlington played with the cuffs of his right-hand sleeve. "What does he hold over you, Miss Darby?"

It was the one question she didn't want to answer, but she knew she had to.

"In private, he has claimed that he can prove my father was involved in the smuggling of goods into England and evading taxes." She hesitated, hoping she could trust Darlington with such information.

"And is he? Guilty, I mean?"

"No! I mean, that is to say, *he* isn't. But I fear the men he invests with might very well be guilty. I believe Milburn might even be working with them to frame my father, and unfortunately I have no way of stopping them. If I marry him, he says he will destroy the evidence, but if I do not..."

"And you believe that an engagement to me will stop him?"

"It has to," she whispered. "If he no longer desires me, then he has no reason to go through with his threats. And you are one of the most wicked men in London. If he isn't afraid of you and tries to take what is yours, such as a future wife, he would be mad."

The corners of lips twitched. "That is certainly true. I wouldn't hesitate to destroy any who dared take what is mine, especially a woman. Very well, I agree to this scheme, mad though it is." Darlington held out one hand to her. "Shall we shake upon it?" He was quite serious, except for the wicked gleam in his eyes. A gleam that promised every moment with him would be deliciously sinful torture.

Perdita placed her palm in his. "We have an accord."

"Agreed." He turned her hand in his, lifting it to his lips as he kissed her knuckles.

"Good." She hesitated, relishing the feel of his lips

upon her bare fingers before she tugged her hand free of his. "My mother is hosting a Christmas party at our estate in Lothbrook. I will see to it that you are invited. Please bring your valet, and have him pack enough clothes to last through Christmas."

Darlington nodded, but when she turned to leave, he caught her arm.

"Yes? Lord Darlington?" She eyed his hand on her arm. He did not release her, not like another man would.

"Given our new intimacy, it would please me to be called Vaughn whenever we are alone."

"Vaughn." She tested the sound of his given name, hating that she liked how smoothly it rolled off her tongue.

"And I expect to be introduced to Lord and Lady Lennox before the end of this year. Will that be possible?"

Perdita nodded. "Yes. I will arrange it as soon as I can."

"Good." He tucked her arm in his. "Let me escort you out."

"Really, my lord—Vaughn. There's no need."

"I need to practice playing the part of a gentleman. I fear I may be a bit rusty."

She remained silent as he led her down the stairs. When he opened the front door, she paused as the bitter wind cut through her. She glanced at him a moment longer before she pulled her cloak hood back up, concealing her features. She rushed to the waiting coach and climbed inside. She chanced one last peek at him through the curtains. He stood there in the doorway without a coat. She remembered the heat of his body pressed to hers and shivered, but not from the cold.

How strange to have made a bargain with Vaughn, Viscount Darlington. They were now bound together, and though they were united in their mission, she felt incredibly alone. She wished she could talk to her dear friend Alexandra, but she was the last person Perdita could confide in when it came to Vaughn.

When Vaughn had kidnapped Alex, it had been a terrifying ordeal, even after Vaughn had revealed he had no intention of harming her. When Alex learned of her supposed engagement to Vaughn, she would no doubt rush to Perdita and try to put a stop to her madness. It was not a meeting Perdita looked forward to, but she and Alex had such different views on how to handle society. Alex had hidden from it while Perdita had embraced it.

Perdita needed Vaughn's dangerous reputation. It was the last shield she had against Samuel Milburn. It was something her dear friend would not understand because she was not the target of Milburn's evil intent. Perdita had sold her soul to a lesser devil to protect herself from a worse one.

She prayed only that their scheme would work, or she was doomed.

CHAPTER 2

Vaughn Darlington watched the coach vanish into the wintry night, his smile fading as the distance between him and Perdita Darby grew. He was a tad melancholy after the whirlwind of the last half hour. Part of him was still amused by the little beauty —her tenacity, her courage, even her recklessness in approaching someone with his reputation in his bedchamber. At midnight, no less.

A proposition, she'd said. And what a proposition it had been. The run of bad luck that had burdened him for so long seemed to be taking a turn for the better, and all because of a little country girl with sound intuition when it came to the darker side of Samuel Milburn.

His smile grew grim. She thought his announced interest in her would put off Milburn, but Vaughn knew Milburn better than she did. Whatever intentions Vaughn had for her, as his mistress or his betrothed, her scheme would not likely matter to a man like Milburn. He was a true bastard, a danger to the fairer sex, and would find a way to claim what he thought was rightfully his.

Yet Vaughn hadn't been able to tell her that whatever he did with her would not be enough to stop Milburn. Not on its own. Vaughn could only hope their little charade would give him a chance to stop whatever Milburn was planning.

He considered the larger problem. Leverage. That was what Milburn had. So long as he held this evidence regarding Miss Darby's father, if it even existed, he would be in a position to pressure and cajole her. First, he would demand she break off her engagement, then bide his time before he held her feet to the fire to accept his own proposal. That sounded like the bastard's style. But without that evidence, his position would crumble.

He would put his butler on it. Craig was far more than he appeared to be, and he had not always been a butler. He had his ways of making men tell the truth. If anyone could get to the bottom of this, it was him.

His thoughts turned back to Perdita and her reaction to the nip he gave her shoulder. While Vaughn was quite notorious for his penchant for pain mixed with pleasure in bed play, he never harmed his bed partners. Milburn, however, had killed his last mistress, or so it was said. The rumors had been murmured in the seediest clubs, and once Vaughn heard he'd been disgusted with the man.

Without proof, there wasn't enough to take the case to court. Milburn, as a gentleman, would escape prosecution.

The affair left a sour taste in Vaughn's mouth, which was why he'd agreed to help Perdita. He knew Milburn and his type. The man would stop at nothing until he was married to her, and then the law would do nothing once her new husband revealed his cruel streak.

Perdita was in danger, and the only way to remedy that was to offer her the ultimate protection—his name given in marriage. It was the reason he had taken so long to give her an answer. She had no idea that what she really needed was a true wedding, not a false engagement. And ordinarily, he would have declined.

But something about Perdita had changed his mind. It had happened ever so subtly over the course of their interaction. The way she'd softened in his arms when he'd kissed her. The way she'd challenged him when he'd reminded her of what her reputation would be like at the end of her charade. The way she was a charming and yet innocent country maiden who responded with fire and bravado. She'd intrigued him even as she'd stormed into his bedchamber, where there was no chaperone to save her from his clutches. None of it had been an act. Perdita was a woman worth knowing, a woman with secrets and passions and a mind all her own. *That* was a woman he could marry.

A smile crept back onto his face, and this time it was one of hesitant joy.

Vaughn walked into the drawing room and approached the tray of drinks his butler had set out earlier. He poured himself a glass of brandy before he took a seat in the chair by the fire just starting to turn to embers. He sipped his drink, savoring the flavor as he contemplated the unique opportunity Perdita had presented him with tonight.

It had been so long since he had looked forward to anything. Ever since his parents had died five years past, he'd been mired in debts that were too deep to recover from on his own. No matter what he did, he seemed to be damned. He'd had to close his country estate, let go of his entire staff save for one caretaker, and reduce the staff at his London townhouse.

His only way of getting by had been to win wagers at the clubs, and even that source was running dry. Every man in every major club now knew better than to wager large stakes when they found him across the gaming table. His ability to win should have helped pay off his family's debts, but not even the most gullible lads were foolish enough to stake their fortunes against him now.

He'd become known as the Devil of London in a matter of months. The moniker hadn't upset him as much as he thought it would at first, but it had kept men from playing even a simple game of cards with him. His friends certainly didn't approve of his actions, and in the last few years most had abandoned him.

Of course, he'd done other things, worse things, to drive his friends away. In the fall he had approached

White's infamous betting book and found a five-thousand-pound sum wagered for publicly seducing a young woman named Alexandra Rockford, Perdita's close friend.

Kidnapping was not at all a charming prospect to him, unless of course the lady *wished* to be kidnapped. He'd played that particular game more than a few times with delightful results, but kidnapping Alexandra had been...*dreadful*.

He indulged in a moment of self-loathing. The night he had taken Alexandra to his home to fake her ruination for the sake of a wager had left a dark stain. He hated himself far more than he ever had before, and it showed how desperate he had truly become. That loathing had deepened until it left a scar on his heart. One he doubted would ever go away.

When he found Perdita in his doorway tonight, he hadn't expected to feel anything. Yet he had. She'd lowered her hood, and her brown hair had turned a burnished bronze in the lamplight. Her eyes, a gentle shade of brown like topaz stones, turned warm as honey. His blood had burned with desire in a way it hadn't in a long while. If that wasn't reason enough to marry the girl, he wasn't sure what else would be.

He left the drawing room and sought out his butler. He found the older man in his office on the basement of the townhouse.

"Mr. Craig, I have a task for you."

The butler glanced up from the papers on his desk. He

gave Vaughn an appraising look. "Am I correct in assuming that this lies outside my usual duties?"

"You are."

Mr. Craig sighed. "I am no longer a young man, my lord."

"This is not for my own selfish desires, Mr. Craig. That young woman you brought to me requires our help. Her very life may depend on it."

Those words seemed to give Mr. Craig new vigor. He rose to his feet like a man twenty years younger. "Name it, my lord."

"A man named Samuel Milburn claims to have evidence that Mr. Reginald Darby has been involved in smuggling and evading taxes. He's using this as a means to pressure Darby's daughter into accepting marriage to him."

Mr. Craig scowled. Though he did not look it, he was at heart a romantic. In fact, Vaughn had caught him reading the works of L. R. Gloucester, a gothic novelist, on more than one occasion. The thought of any man forcing a woman by such means would be anathema to him.

"I want you to look into this. Miss Darby believes her father invested with men who might be working with Milburn. It could be they are trying to lay false evidence that Darby is the one behind the ill deeds. What we need is proof that Milburn is attempting to blackmail the Darby family, or proof of Mr. Darby's innocence. And if at all possible, I want you to put a stop to whoever is causing these problems, if you understand my meaning."

Mr. Craig's grim smile was a reminder of the man he'd once been, a man who'd fought valiantly for his country in the shadows years before.

"Understood."

He rarely spoke of those times, and when he did it was often in an allegorical fashion, but Vaughn had seen on more than one occasion just what Mr. Craig was capable of. And despite his complaints of old age and weariness, it took little to light the old fire under him again.

He left his butler and called for his valet, knowing the fellow would be up late.

"Barnaby!" His voice echoed in the darkened corridor. A few seconds later the man appeared around the edge of the door leading to the servants' quarters.

"My lord?"

"Pack me a valise for at least a week. We're going to Lothbrook in a few days and shall be there for Christmas." He tipped his brandy back and finished it before he headed for the stairs to return to his bedchamber.

Barnaby wrinkled his nose. "Lothbrook again? I'm still scraping the dust out of your trousers from the last visit, my lord." The man muttered this more to himself than to his master. Neither of them cared much for the country. It was so bloody provincial, but if he had to return there to seduce his unknowing bride, then that was where he must go.

He would deal with the details of his travel arrangements in the morning once he had had word from Perdita's parents that he was invited to their estate. With another small smile, he returned to his bedchamber and began to strip down for bed. He always slept in the buff, even in winter. It was a habit that would no doubt shock his little bride-to-be, but he suspected she would shock him right back. He closed his eyes, letting his mind flash images of her as he bent to kiss her, and the memory of it resurrected a smile upon his lips.

Her startled look, then the way she'd melted in his arms. She'd tasted like honey and fire, burning, yet impossibly sweet. He could still feel the velvet of her cloak, crumpled in his hands as he latched on to her. He had wanted to slide his hand up her skirts right then, but that would've been a step too far, no matter how she'd claimed she was not an innocent creature.

She was wanton, he would agree, yet still innocent in so many ways. Introducing Perdita to the mysteries of a man and woman coming together was not a thing to be rushed. Hasty fumblings in the dark would not do. No, she deserved a well-planned, deliciously slow seduction of the body and the mind.

Vaughn sat on the edge of his bed, raking his hands through his hair as he considered his next move. Tomorrow he needed to purchase a ring. He had little money to do so, but he'd find a way. His smile stretched into a broad grin. The invisible forces of fate had seemed determined to stop him from restoring his family's name in the *ton*, and now he had found a way to win against them: marry the *ton*'s darling. Miss Darby was the answer to his prayers. What a shock it would be to them all.

London's sweetest lady mated to its fiercest devil.

PERDITA STOOD BY HER MOTHER'S WRITING DESK IN HER private sitting room, her heart racing more than it ought. Her mother sat at her delicate escritoire and was diligently checking the guest list for the party that would occupy their country estate in a few days. Perdita shifted about, her red shawl dropping from her shoulders to hang about her elbows and lower back.

"Perdita dear, you're lingering. You know how much I detest lingering. Either come and speak to me or be off."

Smoothing the skirts of her pale-rose gown, Perdita approached her mother and cleared her throat.

"I should like to add a guest to the list, Mama, if you don't mind. I know we have extra rooms." The estate was an ancient one that, while lacking the pomp of a peerage family with a title, was still a rival to many of the aristocratic homes in the country. It boasted no less than twenty bedrooms, a ballroom, and a music room. Perdita had numerous unpleasant memories of plucking away at a harp during an arranged musicale performance when she debuted two years ago.

Her mother glanced up, wisps of brown hair threaded with silver creeping out from her turban. "Oh? And who do you wish me to invite?"

Perdita straightened herself. "My fiancé."

The quill in her mother's hand seemed to hover a moment in midair before it clattered flat on the writing desk, splattering ink on the corner of the list her mother had been writing.

"Your..."

"Fiancé. Yes."

Her mother's eyes were as large as saucers. "So you accepted Mr. Milburn, then?"

"Er...no. It is someone else."

"What? But who?"

Perdita understood her mother's shock. It had been two long years since her debut, and she had rejected all offers that first year. The second season she had not received any offers. Rather than become a spinster, she'd cultivated her reputation as a young lady of good character. Debutantes came to her for advice, society mamas sought the name of her modiste, and gentlemen sought her for conversations.

She was well versed to play the role set out for her. Charming and delightful, she was welcome in every London household. The one thing she had *not* done was allow herself to be courted. The men of England had given up, until Samuel Milburn met her a few months ago at a dinner party.

Their encounter had been brief, pointedly cool, at least from Perdita's side. Milburn had taken her cool aloofness in stride and informed her parents the following day of his intentions. Once Perdita learned of this, she'd come up with her desperate plan and had been biding her time until she felt safe enough to go to Vaughn.

"It's Lord Darlington, Mama. He and I have been seeing each other in secret. I know you disapprove of such things, but we wanted to be sure of our affections before we let society pry into our affairs."

Her mother's eyes nearly bulged out of her head. "Darlington? But... Good heavens, what about Milburn? I can't rescind his invitation for Christmas. He was most excited to come shooting with your father."

"I know..." Perdita pretended to consider the dilemma carefully, though she already knew her mind about it. "He must still come. However, we must also extend Lord Darlington an invitation."

Her mother picked up her quill and poised herself to write, but paused. "Are you quite sure, my dear? Lord Darlington is quite wicked, so I hear. I know I teased you in September about pursuing him, but it was only a jest."

"He is a viscount, Mama. His title will further us in society, will it not?"

"It will, but that's no reason to marry a man. If you loved him, that would be one thing, but if you don't, I wouldn't expect you to marry him."

Perdita held her breath, trying to summon the courage

to lie to her mother, a thing she had never liked to do and avoided whenever possible.

"I love him, Mama, and I believe with a bit of time I can tame his restless spirit." She gave her mother an imploring look.

"Well, that is entirely possible, even of the worst rogues. I tamed your father, after all."

There was a loud *harrumph* from the doorway. Perdita turned to see her father standing there. He looked dapper in his blue breeches and waistcoat, his gray mustache twitching as he watched them.

"Tame *me?*" her father chortled. "Woman, you didn't tame me."

"I most certainly did!" Her mother stood, moving from her writing desk and to her husband. "You were a terrible rogue in your day, and it was quite the feat to bring you to your senses."

Perdita watched her parents with a blush in her cheeks.

"I only let you believe that." Her father's eyes twinkled as he caught Perdita's mother by her waist and pulled her close, kissing her cheek.

"Heavens, Reginald!" her mother hissed, but she was smiling as she chastised him. "Not here!"

"Very well." Reginald sighed dramatically. "Now, what's all this about taming men?"

"Well." Her mother waved at Perdita. "Your daughter

seems to have gotten herself engaged and is only just now telling us."

"Milburn asked you, then?" Her father studied her curiously. His gaze was serious rather than delighted that his daughter had just announced she was to be married.

Perdita shook her head. "Um, no, actually. It was Lord Darlington. You remember him, don't you, Papa? He came to the garden party in September and stayed with us for a short time."

Papa raised one dark brow. "Darlington? You don't say…"

"Yes." Perdita's mother would be too blinded by the joy of knowing her child was to be married, but her father was a little more levelheaded and might see through things.

"And you want to bring him for Christmas, is that it? Well, bring the lad so I can measure him and see if he is up to snuff. He ought to have come to me first, like that Milburn fellow did." Her father appeared to look stern, but there was a twinkle in his eyes that made Perdita want to laugh. If only she really were engaged. It was surprising to see how happy she had made her parents.

"We were keeping it a secret until we were sure of ourselves." Perdita pleaded with her eyes, hoping her father believed her. She needed Vaughn to come. She'd tried to mention Samuel Milburn's reputation to her father before, but he'd brushed it aside as idle talk. He knew all too well that gossip had been known to ruin lives unjustly and was disinclined to hear any more about it. It was one of the few times she'd ever been furious with him.

"Hmm, well, invite the boy, then." Her father kissed her mother's cheek and left them alone again.

"Perdita dear, I am most happy for you, of course, but are you quite sure Darlington is the one? I mean, you may have offers again from more than one gentleman. I was worried that..." Her mother trailed off, and heavy silence filled the room. It was only a matter of time before the *ton* tired of her and she was left on the shelf to become a spinster. She did not mind, but she knew her parents wished to see her happily married.

"Vaughn is the one for me." She used his given name purposefully, and it had the desired effect.

"Is it truly a love match? You know I only ever wanted a love match for you. That's why I always invite every young man I can find in hopes he might be perfect for you. Milburn seemed so attentive, and everyone spoke well of him. I had hopes that you might feel the same...but if your heart belongs to Lord Darlington, then that's settled, isn't it?"

Perdita clasped her mother's hands and squeezed them. She was a determined matchmaker for sport, but Perdita knew her mother's intentions were pure. She had married Papa for love and only wanted the same for her daughter. As often as her mother could be exasperating, she was also impossibly wonderful. That was why it hurt so much to lie to her.

"Yes. It is a love match. I never thought I'd win the heart of a man like Vaughn, but somehow I did."

"Win his heart?" Her mother chuckled. "You only need to win his mind first. It is he who must win *your* heart." Her mother squeezed her hands in return. "Very well, I shall invite your darling Darlington." She winked at Perdita and walked back to her desk to resume her guest list.

"If you don't mind, Mama, I am to have tea with Lady Lysandra Russell this afternoon at Gunter's."

"Of course." She returned her focus to her list. "Give her mother my regards, and take a footman with you."

"Thank you, Mama. Don't forget to send Darlington's invitation today. I wanted it to come from you so he would feel welcome."

"Consider it done." Her mother pulled a fresh bit of parchment toward her and began to scratch away with her quill, her turbaned head bowed.

Perdita called for Hensley, one of the young footmen, to bring her cloak and summon a coach. It would be too cold for ices, which Gunter's was most famous for. Tea would be preferable. They would also have to meet indoors. Gunter's was a treat when the weather was fine. A lady could arrive in Berkeley Square and remain in her open carriage while the men rushed from Gunter's to bring ices out to waiting customers. Indoors was perfectly fine for her intentions today. She and Lysandra had important things to discuss.

Hensley met her by the door and held out her dark-blue cloak. She slipped it on and took a white mink muff, tucking her hands inside. Then she and Hensley walked to the coach waiting for them.

When they reached Gunter's, Hensley came inside with her but kept his distance so she might enjoy her time alone with her friend. Lysandra Russell was waiting, a tea service in front of her at one of the tables. Her bright-red hair was like a flame that danced in the lamplight of the shop. Lysandra didn't seem to notice the appreciative stares of the men around them. But that was just how Lysa was, her head buried in books, her mind preoccupied with their shared purpose.

"Lysa." Perdita took an empty chair opposite her friend at the small tea table.

"Oh! Perdita, forgive me." Lysa blushed and raised her head from her stack of letters. She tucked the letters into her lap and poured a cup of tea for her friend.

"Thank you." Perdita slipped the muff off her hands and sipped her tea.

Lysa beamed. "Our paper on the astronomical developments of the last few months is ready for publication. I believe we might be accepted this time." Lysa grinned and nodded at the pen name they had chosen to hide their genders: P. L. Bottomsley.

"I've drafted a proper introduction. Officially, we are a gentleman from Tintagel, Cornwall. I've acquired the use of an address there. There's a man named Mikhail Barinov.

He's agreed to collect any correspondence and deliver it to London first. I believe this time we shall have our ducks in a row. The Astronomy Society of London *must* publish us."

Perdita couldn't help but smile as well. This was her dream—their observations and scientific discoveries published. As ladies and not learned gentleman scholars, their articles had been continually rejected. And so, a ruse had to be devised. The need for it was maddening.

"Brilliant, Lysa." Perdita took the article and reviewed the neatly written words, checking each page carefully. Then she handed it back to Lysa, who tucked it into a leather folio.

"I will submit it on the morrow with the messenger and let you know once I hear if we've been successful."

"Excellent." Perdita glanced around the shop, her eyes taking in the couples having tea. Gunter's was one of the few places in London a lady could meet with a gentleman alone and not worry about scandal or ruination. The door opened with a small bell tinkling as a group of men came in from the cold. Perdita recognized one of them, and her heart pitched straight to her feet.

Samuel Milburn was here.

"Lysa, I'm so sorry, but I must leave immediately." She nodded discreetly at Samuel, who was removing his hat and coat.

Lysa's eyes settled on the man as she nodded. "Of course. Good luck."

Perdita waved Hensley over.

"Miss?" Hensley asked, brushing crumbs from his trousers.

"I'd like to leave. Please have the coach brought around at once."

Hensley pulled his coat on and ducked outside. Perdita carefully walked around the edge of the tea shop, weaving between the couples and tables, trying to keep out of Samuel's sight. She pulled her hood up and reached the door just in time to overhear part of his conversation with the other gentlemen.

"You've still not proposed to the Darby chit yet?" one of the men asked.

Samuel chuckled. "Not officially. I'm waiting for Christmas. Women love that sort of romantic drivel. I also need to make sure she's mine. I have to be able to have her before I make my decision. There's enough fire in her that I believe she'd be a pleasure to break. Have to make sure though. She might be one of those weepy virginal debutantes. Can't have that. I want her to fight me before I break her completely."

His companions laughed, one comparing such "sport" with the hunting of a wild animal.

Milburn sneered. "Indeed, except one must be stuffed before it is mounted, while the other must be mounted in order to be stuffed."

The grating sound of their harsh laughter made Perdita nearly toss up her accounts. She couldn't bear to hear another word. She rushed out into the cold, not caring if the biting wind tore at her face. Samuel's threats were unimaginable. How could the *ton* be so blinded by him not to see his evil? Yet she feared that was the sort of darkness lying in his soul. He was a man with no heart, and he cared for nothing except his own needs. She would not become his victim; she would do anything to escape such evil. Vaughn would be her salvation. She trusted him, something which should have been surprising, yet it did not feel so.

Evil and sorrow left very different shadows on a man's face. Evil was a malignant presence that smothered and strangled the goodness around it. But it was different with sorrow. Vaughn's eyes were painted in shadows of pain and loss. It was a shadow that might someday be vanquished by the rays of the sun. She had glimpsed the hope of it in his eyes when she'd kissed him last night, like sunlight streaking through the parted curtains of a mansion that had been shrouded in darkness for eons. It was foolish, she knew, to take pleasure in knowing their kiss might've lessened his sorrows, whatever they were, but she did.

Perdita looked around for Hensley and saw with some relief the coach was already approaching. She could not wait another minute this close to Samuel. He and his companions had confirmed her worst nightmares.

Thank heavens for Vaughn.

Hensley had their driver stop the coach, and he helped her inside. The velvet cushions were cold, but she sighed in relief when Hensley placed a foot warmer at her feet.

"Where to now, miss?" Hensley asked.

"Home, I suppose." She parted the curtains on the opposite side of the square, but then she held up a hand. "Wait. Stay here. I should like to go to that shop. The one just there."

She pointed at the little jewelry shop across the street. She could have sworn she'd seen Vaughn entering it. Had she been dreaming merely because she was thinking of him just now? There was only one way to find out.

CHAPTER 3

She climbed back out of the coach, heading directly for the row of shops. If it was Vaughn, she needed to tell him what she'd overheard in Gunter's. He had a right to know Samuel's intentions. He might have an idea of how to protect her against the man since Samuel had made it clear he wanted to get her alone.

Hensley closed the coach door behind her and followed her as she passed a milliner's shop and reached the jeweler's. She peered into the windows, which were frosted around the edges from the cold, but she couldn't see Vaughn.

Perhaps he'd gone deeper into the shop. She tugged on the brass door handle. It creaked open, and she slipped inside. The little shop was warm, but a faint musty smell emanated from the shelves where a variety of necklaces hung on stands and both bracelets and rings were displayed in glass cases. It was clear from the designs that these jewelry items were old, not newly fashioned.

Perdita peered around the shop, searching for Vaughn. She paused behind a row of tall shelves, considering the possibility that she'd only seen a gentleman who bore a passing resemblance to him.

A voice came from the other side of the wall of jewels behind which Perdita stood. "My lord, what may I do for you?"

Perdita perked up at the sound and was prepared to seek out the jeweler, but something held her back. She stayed hidden and peered between the dusty shelves, fighting the need to sneeze with one hand. She glimpsed an elderly shopkeeper with a hooked nose and spectacles speaking with a tall man with dark-blond hair. The man stood with his back to her, but Perdita was positive it was Vaughn.

"What can I get for this?" Vaughn held out a pocket watch, a very old but beautiful piece. Its silver cover glinted with light as it swung from a fine chain. The jeweler took it and held it up, leaving Vaughn to shift slightly. His face turned away from the jeweler, offering Perdita a glimpse of his profile and the pain etched in his features.

"Well now, let me take a look." The jeweler paused to push his glasses up the bridge of his nose and studied the watch closely.

"Finely made, with the Darlington family crest... Forty

pounds, I should think. Are you quite sure you want to part with it, my lord?" The jeweler eyed the watch and then Vaughn. Perdita held her breath. Hensley shifted behind her, and she threw out a hand, catching his arm and raising her other hand to her lips to indicate silence. She did not want to interrupt whatever Vaughn was doing.

It appeared as though he was selling off his family heir-looms. Given the condition of his home—the lack of furnishings and general disrepair—it shouldn't have surprised her. However, if she was being honest, she didn't want to think of Vaughn as so destitute he was selling such a personal item. Her heart gave a painful twinge as she held her breath, listening.

"Forty? I suppose that's a fair enough price. Is there a ring which I might trade it for?" Vaughn set the pocket watch on the counter between him and the jeweler. His fingers didn't immediately let go of the watch. Perdita's heart gave another painful jerk. He was looking at rings? Why would he wish to sell a watch for a ring?

Then a thought struck her. Was the ring for her?

The jeweler lifted a velvet box onto the counter. "These here are quite lovely." Perdita stood on tiptoe to get a better view. She was thankful the shelves were open for her to peer through.

"This one here, is it a ruby?" Vaughn pointed at a ring. She couldn't see which because his body was blocking her view.

"Yes, a fine ruby. I suppose we could make a fair trade for the watch," the jeweler said.

"Good." Vaughn nudged the watch toward him. "Do you have a box for it?"

"I do." The jeweler disappeared into the back and moments later emerged with a small blue velvet box. He placed the ring inside and handed it back to Vaughn.

"Thank you." Vaughn took the box and tucked it securely into his coat and lifted his hat off the counter.

"Good day, my lord," the jeweler said as Vaughn turned toward the door—and Perdita. Perdita grasped Hensley and propelled him around the opposite end of the shelf, just missing being seen by Vaughn as he left. Once she was sure Vaughn was no longer inside, she and Hensley moved around the shelf and approached the counter where Vaughn had stood. The jeweler was still putting the set of rings back beneath the glass display counter.

"Oh! Good day, miss" the jeweler said. "I didn't realize you'd come in. How may I assist you?" He brushed his hands on his apron and readjusted his glasses with a warm smile.

Perdita noticed Vaughn's watch still sitting on the counter and tried to act slightly interested. "This is a lovely watch. May I see it?" she asked.

The jeweler eyed her quizzically. "The old pocket watch?"

She nodded, chancing one glance at the door. There was no sign of Vaughn returning.

"Of course." The jeweler set the watch down on the counter so Perdita could examine it. It was indeed an old watch, possibly Vaughn's father's or even his grandfather's. How could he bear to part with it? For a ring, no less?

She hadn't thought what it meant to provide evidence to support their story of an engagement. Had Vaughn believed he needed proof such as this? Or was it for a mistress? For some reason, she didn't think so. If he was as destitute as she now believed, he could not afford a mistress. That left her with the sad knowledge that the ring must be for her, and he had sold his watch for it. She had to buy it back. He had sold the watch, one she suspected was dear to him, for a ring she believed he meant to give to her. Therefore, she would make sure he got his watch back when the time was right. Vaughn was a proud man, and she would not endanger his pride by letting him know she'd witnessed this moment.

"How much for it?"

"Pardon, miss?" The jeweler's brows rose.

"How much to buy the watch? I'd like to buy it." She didn't want Vaughn to lose one of the last pieces of his family's past if she could help it.

"Well...I believe fifty pounds is fair."

She met his gaze. "But you traded it for forty."

"Forty-five then," the jeweler countered.

She lifted her chin. "Forty-two."

The jeweler stuck out his chin as well. "Forty-three."

"Agreed." She lifted her reticule onto the counter and

LAUREN SMITH

counted out the notes. She rarely carried large sums of money, but she had planned to do a bit of shopping today after meeting with Lysandra. She hadn't expected it to be for her false fiancé.

She had the jeweler wrap it for her and then entrusted the box to Hensley.

"We're going home now, miss?" His hesitant tone implied his hope at the thought.

"Not a lover of clandestine meetings or secret missions, Hensley?" she teased. The footman, a man close to her age, blushed to the roots of his hair.

"It isn't that, miss... I just worry about you, is all."

The footman's honest comment caught her off guard.

"Worry about me?" she asked. He was unable to meet her eyes.

"I shouldn't have said that, miss. My apologies." He continued to avoid her gaze, and she didn't force him to speak of it further. Mostly because she was afraid to hear what he would say. There was an infuriating pity that came from servants when they dealt with spinsters, as though even downstairs they felt sorry for the unmarried maids who aged on the shelf.

The thought made her sour. Women had a right to aspire to other positions than simply being a wife and mother, did they not? Yet those were the only positions society valued for them. It wasn't her fault she didn't wish to be seen as a broodmare. The idea filled her with a defiant purpose. Once she and Vaughn were done with this charade and Milburn had lost interest, she would devote herself to seeing her astronomy essays published.

"We have one more stop to make," Perdita announced. "Have the driver take us to Half Moon Street." Then she climbed into the coach and listened for Hensley to give orders to the driver.

She peered eagerly out of the coach window as they reached Lennox House. It was a stunningly built structure that emanated both power and beauty. Her warm breath clouded the glass. She rubbed her gloved hand on the window to remove some of the fog for a better look.

The coach came to a stop, and Perdita instructed Hensley to wait with the driver for her. Depending on how furious her friend Rosalind was at her request, it was possible Perdita would be cast back into the street. A small bout of nerves rose up in her, but she shoved them down. The two were friends, and although she had not had a chance to visit Rosalind since she'd married Lord Lennox and moved into his house, things shouldn't have changed much, or so she hoped.

She rapped the large silver knocker and waited. The butler answered, and she was relieved to be allowed in once he had made the proper inquiries.

The butler directed her to a drawing room. Rosalind was working at a writing desk by the fire.

"Perdita." Rosalind rose once she entered the room. "How are you?" Her voice lilted with a Scottish accent, one she no longer tried to hide as much as she used to.

The accent rendered the dark-haired woman utterly charming with a touch of that Highland wildness.

"I am well, and you?"

"Very well." Rosalind's gray eyes twinkled. "Have you come to discuss your investments?"

"Yes, well, possibly. It is a matter of business, but it is also a bit delicate in nature."

Her friend's open smile turned to a frown. "Shall we sit?" Rosalind led her to a dark-red brocade settee and poured a cup of tea from a pot on the table.

"Thank you." Perdita steeled herself for what she had to do. It was not like her to make such requests of friends.

Rosalind seemed to notice her hesitation. "We are friends, Perdita. Ask whatever you came to ask."

"It is a rather long tale, but I shall try to be brief. I'm trying to escape an engagement to Samuel Milburn, whose intentions I do not trust. I do not wish to go into details, but I am under some rather unsavory pressure to accept. I made a bargain with Viscount Darlington to act as my fiancé in order to put Milburn off. But Darlington's price in aiding me is..." She choked on the words, hating to have to speak this way to a friend. "Well, his fortunes have taken a poor turn, and he wishes me to ask for your husband to involve him in his next investment." There. She'd said it, even though it left a bitter taste upon her tongue.

For a long moment, Rosalind didn't speak, her brows furrowed as she studied Perdita carefully. Did she think

Perdita was only trying to use her? Was she reconsidering their friendship?

"Darlington, you say?" Rosalind pursed her lips and thought. "I haven't met him, but I've heard of him. Bit of a wild fellow. Are you sure you want to attach yourself to him so publicly?"

Perdita sipped her tea and nodded. "Despite what you may have heard of Samuel Milburn, I assure you that man is a brute. He has every intention of breaking me if he can compromise me into marriage."

"*Break* you?"

"My spirit, and perhaps more."

Rosalind's pensive gaze turned into a scowl. "I haven't heard much about this Milburn fellow, but if he has you frightened, we shan't let him succeed in putting you in a position where you must marry him." She lifted a small bell from her tea tray and rang it. A footman appeared, and Rosalind spoke. "Please tell my husband I wish to speak with him."

The servant bowed and vanished.

"Is there really no way other than to enlist Lord Darlington's help? I'm sure you've heard the rumors about him," Rosalind said.

"I have, but I believe there may be more to him than the rumors give him credit for. When presented with a situation such as I have given him, he wished to help and asked only this favor in return. It's not what I expected of a notorious rogue, but I trust him. Does that sound very strange and foolish?"

"To trust a rogue? That is neither strange nor foolish, if it's the right rogue. I will ask my husband what he knows of Darlington."

"Thank you, Rosalind. I cannot tell you how much I appreciate your help. It's so upsetting to have to ask it of you."

"Nonsense. This is precisely what friends are for." Rosalind covered Perdita's hand and gave it a gentle pat.

Lord Lennox appeared a moment later. He was a tall man with piercing blue eyes and blond hair, not unlike Vaughn, but there was a wild desperation to Vaughn that Lennox did not share. He was calm, relaxed, *settled*. Vaughn had a leaner appearance to him and a grimness to his bearing that gave him a melancholy darkness.

"You summoned me?" While Ashton's tone was cool, his lips were curled in a teasing smile. He came over to Rosalind and pressed a kiss to her hand.

"This is my dear friend, Perdita Darby. She is also a customer of our bank," Rosalind explained. "Perdy, please tell my husband what you told me."

Perdita detailed what she had guessed of Samuel Milburn and his intentions, as well as her scheme with Darlington and the favor required as payment for his services.

"I've met him a few times around London. Not a bad fellow, or so I hear," Lennox mused. "Milburn, on the other hand...well, I've heard about his mistress. The one who fell to her death. An accident, they say, but I'm not sure I believe that."

Perdita nodded.

"So, Darlington is keen to invest with me?" Ashton leaned back in his chair thoughtfully. "He wouldn't be the first, but there are good reasons why I am selective about whom I take into my confidence. Most believe the risks I take are too great, but they simply do not understand my longer plans and fail to see that in the end there is very little risk at all. But I require trust, and not all are willing to give it. I will not have my every action second-guessed. I believe he'd make a good partner. He has a good head on his shoulders, and I understand he was quite successful before his parents passed. The debts they left him with were extraordinary and ruined his own small fortune."

Lennox shared a long glance with Rosalind before he stood and nodded.

"Very well, tell Darlington he may call upon me after the New Year. I shall discuss my next venture with him, and he can decide then if he still wishes to take part."

His words were such a relief that Perdita was overcome with gratitude. "Thank you, Lord Lennox. Truly."

"Any friend of Rosalind's is a friend of mine." He kissed her hand, and with a lingering glance at his wife, which made the lady blush, he left them alone.

"Silly man," Rosalind muttered, though she was smiling.

Perdita had to agree. Lord Lennox was a silly, wonderful man. *Wait until I tell Vaughn. He'll be so pleased.* She had guaranteed not just an introduction, but involvement in Lennox's next venture. Perhaps she would survive Christmas after all.

Want to know what happens next? Grab the book HERE! For print readers, please visit your favorite bookstore to order a copy.

OTHER TITLES BY LAUREN SMITH

Historical
The League of Rogues Series
Wicked Designs
His Wicked Seduction
Her Wicked Proposal
Wicked Rivals
Her Wicked Longing
His Wicked Embrace (coming soon)
The Earl of Pembroke (coming soon)
His Wicked Secret (coming soon)
The Seduction Series
The Duelist's Seduction
The Rakehell's Seduction
The Rogue's Seduction (coming soon)
Standalone Stories

Tempted by A Rogue
Sins and Scandals
An Earl By Any Other Name
A Gentleman Never Surrenders
A Scottish Lord for Christmas

Contemporary
The Surrender Series
The Gilded Cuff
The Gilded Cage
The Gilded Chain
Her British Stepbrother
Forbidden: Her British Stepbrother
Seduction: Her British Stepbrother
Climax: Her British Stepbrother

Paranormal
Dark Seductions Series
The Shadows of Stormclyffe Hall
The Love Bites Series
The Bite of Winter
Brotherhood of the Blood Moon Series
Blood Moon on the Rise (coming soon)
Brothers of Ash and Fire
Grigori: A Royal Dragon Romance
Mikhail: A Royal Dragon Romance (coming soon)
Rurik: A Royal Dragon Romance (coming soon)

Sci-Fi Romance
Cyborg Genesis Series
Across the Stars (coming soon)

Lauren
SMITH
TIMELESS ROMANCE

ABOUT THE AUTHOR

Lauren Smith is an Oklahoma attorney by day, author by night who pens adventurous and edgy romance stories by the light of her smart phone flashlight app. She knew she was destined to be a romance writer when she attempted to re-write the entire *Titanic* movie just to save Jack from drowning. Connecting with readers by writing emotionally moving, realistic and sexy romances no matter what time period is her passion. She's won multiple awards in several romance subgenres including: New England Reader's Choice Awards, Greater

Detroit BookSeller's Best Awards, and a Semi-Finalist award for the Mary Wollstonecraft Shelley Award.

To Connect with Lauren, visit her at:
www.laurensmithbooks.com
lauren@laurensmithbooks.com